SUITABLE BRIDE

RAFAEL'S
SUITABLE BRIDE

BY

CATHY WILLIAMS

MILLS & BOON®
Pure reading pleasure™

First published in Great Britain 2008
Large Print edition 2009
Harlequin Mills & Boon Limited,
Eton House, 18-24 Paradise Road,
Richmond, Surrey TW9 1SR

© Cathy Williams 2008

ISBN: 978 0 263 20572 5

Set in Times Roman 16½ on 19 pt.
16-0309-55040

Printed and bound in Great Britain
by CPI Antony Rowe, Chippenham, Wiltshire

CHAPTER ONE

ON A day when most sane people were doing their utmost to stay off the roads, Rafael Rocchi had decided against the ease and speed of the train and chosen instead to bring his Ferrari out of hiding. It wasn't often that he got the opportunity to drive it, and what was the point of having all that supercharged brake horsepower and black metal tucked away in his London garage—cleaned and polished once a week by his chauffeur, Thomas, and then patted gently on the bonnet and locked away for another week of rest and relaxation?

Driving to his mother's house in the Lake District would be perfect. He would be able to lose himself in the sheer pleasure of being behind the wheel of a car that was as powerful and challenging as an unbridled wild horse. Nothing topped it for a sense of freedom, which was, to him, invaluable because by contrast, his day-to-day life was so structured. Running the Rocchi empire, which he had done singlehandedly since his father had died eight years previously, was not exactly a liberating experience. Invigorating, yes. Highly charged and immensely satisfying, yes. Liberating, no.

Once on the open road, the car devoured the distance noiselessly and effortlessly. On this rare occasion, Rafael had switched off his mobile phone and instead was listening to the rousing dynamism of classical music, keenly alert to the condition of the roads, but not unduly bothered. The past few days had seen snow cover the length and breadth of the country, and although none was currently falling, the fields as he headed up north were still blanketed in white.

At no point did he think that a fast car on treacherous roads was a lethal combination. He was utterly convinced of his own ability to control his Ferrari, just as he was convinced of his ability to control every aspect of his life. It was probably why, at the age of thirty-six, he was already legendary in the business world, feared for his ruthlessness as much as for his brilliance.

He was even occasionally inclined to think that women feared him equally, and that, he thought, was a good thing. A little fear never hurt anyone, and it paid to make sure that a woman knew who controlled the strings in a relationship. If six-month flings could be deemed relationships. His mother certainly had an alternative way of describing them, which, he thought, was behind this grand party of hers. A little impromptu post-Christmas event, she had told him, to lift everyone's spirits because there was no month flatter than February—yet how impromptu could a party be when catering for over a hundred people had to be arranged?

No, his mother was on the matchmaking band-wagon again, even though he had repeatedly told her that he was not up for grabs, that he liked his life precisely as it was. As far as his mother was concerned—traditional Italian that she still was at heart, even after decades of living in England—unmarried and offspring-free at the age of thirty-six couldn't possibly be a happy situation for anyone. She herself had married at twenty-two and had had Rafael by twenty-five, and would have had several more children had fate not seen fit to deny her the chance.

She had also insisted that he attend, which was ominous, but in the whole world the one person whom Rafael respected unconditionally was his mother. And so here he was, at least for the moment enjoying the experience of getting there even if, once there, he would be bored out of his skull—and probably stuck having to make mind-numbingly dull small talk with a girl with whom he would almost certainly have nothing in common.

His mother had never come to grips with the truth that Rafael liked his women almost solely for their looks. He liked them tall, blonde, obliging and, most important of all, temporary.

All it took was that small lull in his concentration. As he rounded the corner of the small country road which led towards his mother's substantial property, he pressed on the brakes at the sight of a car which had veered off the road and ploughed into the snowy bank at the side. The Ferrari spun round, and in a squeal of protesting tyres came to a halt just feet away from the hapless and, as Rafael could see as soon as he had stormed out of his skewed car, abandoned Mini.

His pleasurable satisfaction had come to an abrupt halt, and there was someone on whom he could vent his well-deserved rage. Someone standing up from the other side of the Mini now, fixing him with a startled glance. A woman. Typical.

'What the hell's going on here? Are you hurt?'

The woman stepped out and blinked up at him.

'Well?' Rafael demanded. As an afterthought, he realised that he had better move his car just in case someone else rounded the corner. The road was always deserted, but there was no point taking chances.

'I have to move my car,' he told the woman who didn't appear to have a tongue in her head.

When he next stepped out of his now parked car, it was to find that she had disappeared once again.

With mounting irritation, Rafael walked round the back of the Mini and found her kneeling on the ground, looking for something with the help of the light from her mobile phone.

'Sorry,' came an anxious apology from the squatting figure. 'I'm really sorry. Are you all right?' A quick glance in his direction, then the search for whatever was missing began again.

'Have you any idea how dangerous it is for you to leave your car there?' He nodded curtly at the Mini.

'I tried moving it, honestly, but the tyres kept squealing.' She stood up, reluctantly abandoning her search, and chewed her lips nervously.

Rafael could now see that the woman in question was little over five-three. Short and dumpy from the looks of it. Which did nothing for his diminishing patience levels. Had she been willowy and beautiful, his charm-gene might have automatically been kick-started. As it was, he looked down at her with a frown of displeasure.

'So you then decided to leave it where it lay, never mind the risk you were causing to anyone coming round the bend, and start scrabbling on the road instead?' His voice was laced with sarcasm. Never noted for high levels of patience, Rafael was now on the verge of snapping completely.

'Actually, I wasn't scrabbling on the road. I was… I rubbed my eyes to wake myself up, and one of my contact lenses came out. I've been driving all the way from London. I should have taken the train, but I want to leave first thing in the morning and I didn't want to be rude and have to wake anyone up to drop me to the station.' She looked up at him earnestly. 'Hello, by the way.' She held out one small hand and stared at the stranger.

He was the most beautiful stranger she had ever seen in her entire life. Actually, he could have stepped off the cover of a magazine. He was very tall, over six feet, and his dark hair was combed back so that there was nothing to distract from the perfect chiselled beauty of his face. His scowling face.

Cristina couldn't stop herself from smiling help-lessly, unfazed by his unsympathetic expression.

Rafael ignored the outstretched hand. 'I'll get your car into a less hazardous position and then you'd better get in my car. I assume you're heading in the same direction as me. There's only one house at the end of his lane.'

'Oh, you don't have to do that,' Cristina said breathlessly.

'No, I don't, but I will because I don't want the hassle of dealing with a guilty conscience if you get behind the wheel of your car when you can't see anything and crash.' He spun round on his heels while Cristina continued to watch, with fascinated interest, as he expertly did what she had spent half an hour trying and failing to do.

'That was brilliant,' she told him honestly when he was back in front of her, and Rafael felt some of his anger begin to subside.

'Hardly brilliant,' he muttered. 'But at least the damn thing's in a safer position now.'

'I could drive myself now,' Cristina was forced to admit. 'I mean, I have a pair of specs in my bag. I always carry them because I never know when my contact lenses are going to start irritating my eyes. Do you wear contact lenses?'

'What?'

'Never mind.' She frowned slightly, belatedly considering her appearance and what lay ahead of her.

'Well?' Rafael was back by his car, passenger door open, waiting for her to stop dithering at the side of the road while the wind whipped around them, reminding them that yet more snow was just a frosted breath away.

Cristina took a couple of steps towards him, her expression still anxious and hesitant. 'It's just that…well…' She spread her hands tellingly along the length of her body. 'Look at me. I can't possibly make an entrance looking like this.' She barely knew her hostess, Maria. She had met her a few times in Italy, when she had been living with her parents before moving to London, and she had seemed a nice lady, but she really wasn't close enough to her to enlist her help in getting cleaned up because she had somehow managed to lose a contact lens. Now her hands were dirty from rummaging on the ground, her tights were torn and she dared not even think of the state of her hair, which was unruly at the best of times.

'Don't be ridiculous,' Rafael told her dismissively. He pulled open the passenger door and sighed impatiently. 'It is freezing out here, and I'm not standing having a prolonged conversation with you about the state of your appearance.' He kindly decided not to point out that there was very little she could have done with her appearance which would have made her look sexy anyway. She was built like a little round ball, and the wind was doing some very unflattering things to her hair. Grubby hands weren't exactly going to go a long way to remedy what looked like a pretty plain gene pool.

However, as she seemed rooted to the spot in

some kind of agony of embarrassment and indecision, and as he was getting colder and colder and more and more impatient by the second, Rafael decided on the only possible solution.

'Get your things from your car and I'll make sure we go through the back entrance. Then I'll take you up to one of the guest suites and you can do whatever it is you think you have to do.'

'Really?' The way he had handled her little car! And now the way he was taking charge, hitting upon a solution to the thorny problem of her appearance! Cristina couldn't help but admire his ingenuity and consideration in helping her out. True, he wasn't exactly giving off sympathetic vibes, but as she hurried to get her overnight bag and coat from her car she decided that that was perfectly understandable. He had, after all, just had the fright of his life when he had taken the corner and nearly crashed into her car.

'Hurry up.' Rafael glanced at his watch and realised that the party would already be in full swing. He had promised his mother that he would make it well in advance, but naturally the demands of work had progressively eaten away into his good intentions.

'You're very kind,' Cristina told him as he took her bag and coat from her and tossed them into the trunk—the virtually invisible-to-the-naked-eye trunk.

Rafael couldn't remember the last time he had been described as kind, and he really wasn't sure that he cared for it, but he shrugged and didn't say anything, just turning the ignition so that his powerful beast of a car roared into immediate life.

'How are you going to find your way to the back entrance?'

At this point in time, Rafael didn't feel inclined to go into his relationship with the hostess. The woman obviously didn't have a clue as to his identity and he preferred to keep it that way. At least for the moment. He had met enough women in his lifetime who'd found his wealth an aphrodisiac. Sometimes it was amusing. Mostly it was just plain dull.

'I never got your name,' he said, changing the conversation, and as his eyes slid over to her he saw the colour flood her cheeks and she looked at him with mortified consternation.

'Cristina. Golly, I'm so rude! You've just rescued me and I haven't even had the wit to introduce myself!' Was she gaping? She thought she might be, and she made an effort to pull herself together and start acting like the twenty-four-year-old woman that she was.

However all attempts at sophistication were ambushed by her intrinsically cheerful personality and impressionable nature. She had met hordes of men throughout her life. That had all been part and parcel of her privileged upbringing in Italy, and then later staying with her aunt in Somerset when she had gone to boarding school. But her experiences with them on any kind of intimate level were limited. Indeed, non-existent, and so the cynicism that came from broken hearts and ruined relationships, which most women would have considered just another part of growing up, had failed to materialise. She had an unbounding faith in the goodness of human nature and was therefore undaunted by Rafael's unwelcoming response to her chatter.

'What's your name?' she asked curiously, abandoning the struggle not to feast her eyes on him.

'Rafael.'

'And how do you know Maria?'

'Why are you so concerned about what kind of

impression you make? Do you know the crowd who are going to be there?'

'Well, no… But… I just can't bear the thought of walking into a roomful of people with torn tights and hair all over the place.' She looked at her hands and sighed. 'My nails are a mess as well, and I especially had a manicure yesterday.' She could feel tears begin to well at her ruined appearance and she stoutly swallowed them back. Instinct told her that here was a man who probably wouldn't welcome the sight of a strange woman howling in his car.

But she had tried so hard. New in London and still without any solid friendships, Maria's invitation had been something lovely to look forward to, and she had really tried to dress for the occasion. Hard as her mother had laboured over the years, in her own sweetly loving way Cristina had always been guiltily aware that she had never managed to live up to the position into which she had been born. Her two sisters, both now married and in their thirties, had been blessed with the sort of good looks that needed very little work. They had been super clothes horses and then, in due course, super wives and super mothers.

She, on the other hand, had blithely failed to live up to expectation. She had grown up a tomboy, more interested in football and playing in the vast gardens of her parents' house than in frocks, make-up and all things girlish. Later, she had developed a love of all things to do with nature and had spent many a teenage summer following around their gardener, asking questions about plants, keenly interested in what could grow where and why. Somewhere along the line she suspected that her mother had given up on her mission to turn her youngest into a lady.

She had distinct concerns about the state of her frock.

'I don't know what possessed me to think that I could find a contact lens on the ground,' she confided glumly.

'Especially with some dregs of snow still left lying about,' Rafael felt obliged to point out.

'Especially,' Cristina agreed. She looked at her knees. 'Torn tights, and I haven't brought a replacement pair. I don't suppose you have a spare lot lying around somewhere…?'

Rafael glanced across at her and saw that she was grinning at him. Well, she certainly had good powers of recovery, he admitted to himself, not to mention a vibrant ability to overlook the fact that he clearly didn't feel inclined to spend the rest of the short trip chatting to her about the state of her appearance.

'Not the sort of thing I usually travel with,' he said seriously. 'Maybe my— Maybe there's a spare pair somewhere in the house…'

'Oh, Maria's probably got drawers full of them, but we're not exactly built along the same lines, are we? She's tall and elegant and I'm, well, I've inherited my father's figure. My sisters are exactly the opposite. They're very long and leggy.'

'And that makes you jealous?' Rafael heard himself asking.

Cristina laughed. It was an unexpectedly infectious sound, something between a guffaw and a giggle—unlike most women who thought that tittering was the ladylike thing to do.

'Lord, no! I mean, I love them to pieces, but I wouldn't swap my life for theirs, not a bit of it. I mean, five kids between them and so much socialising! They're forever having dinner parties and cocktail parties, and entertaining clients at the theatre or the opera. They live quite close to

one another and they're both married to businessmen, you see, which means that they're
always on show. Can you imagine—never being
able to leave the house without a full layer of
make-up and matching accessories?'

Since the women Rafael dated never left the
bedroom without a full layer of make-up and
matching accessories, he could well understand
the lifestyle.

Ahead of him, he could see his mother's house,
a sprawling country mansion of faded yellowing
stone, its chimneys proudly rising upwards and
the front courtyard full of cars, as was the long
drive leading up. Even in the darkness it was
easy to appreciate the grace and symmetry of the
building, and he waited for the predictable gasp
of awe, but none was forthcoming.

This was mildly surprising because he had occasionally brought one of his girlfriends to the
house in the past and roughly about now, as the
house unfolded itself in all its perfect splendour,
they had exclaimed in delight as if on cue.

When he looked he saw that Cristina was fid-
geting with the hem of her dress and the little
frown was back on her face.

'There are an awful lot of cars,' she commented nervously. 'I'm really surprised there's such a good turnout, considering the weather.' Surprised, and a bit dismayed. She disliked big social occasions at the best of times, but this had all the hallmarks of being a vast one.

'People up here are of the hardy variety,' Rafael pointed out. 'Londoners are altogether softer.'

'Is that where you live?'

Rafael nodded and quickly circled the courtyard, and then edged his car down the side-slip towards the back of the house and the tradesman's entrance.

'I thought you might have lived around here,' Cristina said vaguely. 'I thought perhaps that might be how you know the house and stuff.' She tried to carry the observation through to its logical conclusion, but her mind was leaping ahead to the small problem of getting herself cleaned up and presentable for the number of people inside—not to mention Maria, who had been kind enough to invite her along. She might lack the polish of her sisters, but embarrassing her host would be anathema.

The back entrance was, to her relief, considerably less busy. Just the staff to get past.

'I ought to tell you that I'm Maria's son.' Rafael killed the engine and turned towards her.

'Are you?' Cristina looked at him in silence for a few seconds. She was thinking that Maria was a lovely, kind and genuine woman, and kind and genuine people tended to have kind and genuine offspring. She gave him a beaming smile because she realised that, however curt his outward attitude might appear, he was as kind as she had initially judged him to be. 'Your mother's a wonderful person.'

'I'm glad you think so. On that one thing we at least agree.' Without giving her time to respond to that ambiguous statement, he let himself out of the car and proceeded to help her out, while a man, who seemed to have materialised out of thin air raced out to get the bags. This could only mean that his mother had requested a lookout for her tardy son, which was a bit of a bother, considering he was now a reluctant knight in shining armour who had to somehow shuffle his unexpected cargo up the stairs and into one of the guest suites—whichever one was unoccupied, because he suspected a fair few people would be staying over.

He had a few quick words with Eric, the man who had been taking care of everything to do with the house for as long as Rafael could remember, and then signalled to Cristina.

In the remorseless light of the back hallway, he was surprised to see that she wasn't actually the unremittingly plain woman he had first thought.

Of course, no one could call her beautiful. She was way too… He rooted around in his head for a suitable adjective and opted for 'stout'…not precisely fat, but solidly built. The sort who could probably pack a mean punch if the occasion demanded, although a less aggressive person he could hardly have hoped to find. Her face was open and warm, and although she was still looking nervous he could tell that she would be someone given to easy laughter.

And she had enormous eyes, huge liquid-brown eyes, like a spaniel puppy.

In fact, Rafael thought, she was the human equivalent of a spaniel puppy. The direct antithesis to the languid greyhound sort he favoured. But, hell, a deal was a deal and he had promised to help her out with her predicament.

'Follow me,' he said abruptly, and he began

leading her out of the kitchen, and through a myriad back rooms which lay between them and the sound of voices and laughter that signalled the party happening at the front of the house.

Of course, the house was far too big for his mother after his father had died, but she wouldn't hear of having it sold.

'I'm not yet decrepit, Raffy,' she had told him. 'When I need to use stair lifts, then I'll consider selling it.' Knowing his mother, that day would never come. She was as energetic in her early sixties as she had been in her early forties, and although there were wings of the house which were rarely used many of the rooms were taken up at various points of the year by friends and relatives staying over.

Rafael now led Cristina to one of the less-used wings and quickly ushered her into a bedroom suite, where she proceeded to look at him with a mournful expression.

'Oh, for God's sake, woman.' He shook his head and favoured her with a direct and assessing look.

'I know I'm being a nuisance,' Cristina said on a sigh, 'But…' Then she saw the expression on his face and flushed. 'I know I haven't got a perfect figure…' she stuttered in embarrassment. It occurred to her that a man who looked like him, a man whose amazing looks could stop a woman dead in her tracks, would only ever associate himself with his female equivalent—which would probably not be a vertically and horizontally challenged twenty-four-year-old inexperienced woman.

'I've been on countless diets,' she blurted out into the ever-growing silence, 'You wouldn't believe. But like I said, I have my father's shape.' She laughed a pitch higher than was necessary and then subsided into embarrassed silence.

'Your dress has a tear.'

'What? No! Oh, goodness…where?'

Before she could bend to scrutinise her treacherous garment, Rafael was in front of her, then kneeling like a supplicant, holding up the flimsy fabric of her loose, tunic-styled silk dress which, with its cluttered pattern of red and white tiny flowers against a black background, should have been more than up to the job of camouflaging a tear. Unfortunately, as he held it up, the rip seemed to expand in girth until it was all she could see with horrified eyes.

Through her horror, though, she was very much aware of the delicate brush of his fingers against her leg. It sent a thrilling, wicked shiver straight through her body.

'See?'

'What am I going to do?' she whispered.

They looked at each other and Rafael sighed. 'What else did you bring?' Since when had he been in the habit of rescuing damsels in distress?

'Jeans, jumpers, wellies just in case I wanted to have a walk and look around the garden. I absolutely love looking around gardens. I'm addicted to it. The most boring people can sometimes have wonderfully creative streaks that come out in the way they landscape their lawns. I'm babbling, sorry, getting away from the point…which is that I have absolutely nothing appropriate to wear…'

Rafael had never met a woman who only packed the bare necessities. For a few seconds he was reduced to stunned silence, then he reluctantly told her that he would fish something out of his mother's wardrobe. She had enough outfits to clothe most of Cumbria.

'But she's so much taller than me!' Cristina wailed. 'And skinnier!'

But he was already striding out of the room, leaving her to wallow in a very unaccustomed sense of self-pity.

He returned some ten minutes later holding various assorted clothes, all of which seemed hideously bright, not at all suited to someone of a more robust persuasion.

'Right. I can't waste much time here, so strip.'

'What?' Cristina's eyes widened and she wondered, fleetingly, whether she had heard correctly.

'Strip. I brought some…some forgiving items…but you'll have to try them on and you'll have to be quick about it. I'm late enough as it is.'

'I can't…not with you there…watching…'

'Nothing I haven't seen before,' he drawled, amused by her sudden attack of prudishness.

Cristina, however, refused to budge and he waited, looking at his watch while she tried on the armful of clothes in the privacy of the adjoining bathroom.

He could, he knew, always leave her to get on with it. After all, she wasn't his problem. But he found himself staying anyway, and when she finally emerged he swung round, ready to tell her whatever she wanted to hear. Anything to get going with the evening, because he had work to do and would have to disappear virtually as soon as he appeared.

He looked at her and stared before muttering the statutory, 'Looks very nice…'

He hadn't quite expected this. Yes, she was far from willowy, but neither was she as overweight as the dress had suggested. In fact, there was a definite sign of curves, and her breasts were bountiful, barely restrained by the stretchy lilac fabric. She had the golden colouring of someone brought up in kinder climes, and her shoulders, left bare by the sleeveless style of the dress, were rounded but firm. For the first time in memory he was awkwardly conscious of fumbling for something further to say, and avoided the dilemma by opening the door and standing back to let her through.

'Thanks.' Cristina gave him a sincerely felt look of gratitude, then on impulse she tiptoed and kissed him chastely on the cheek.

It was as if she had suddenly been touched with an electric spark. She could actually feel her skin go hot, and it was like nothing she had ever experienced in her life before. She pulled back at roughly the same time as he did and preceded him out of the room, babbling yet again about nothing in particular because she didn't want him to see how hot and bothered she felt.

It was almost a relief to make their way downstairs and to be greeted by the babble of voices, providing her with a comforting backdrop into which she could conveniently slide.

But not until she made her presence known to Maria, who was fussing over a tray of drinks being carried precariously by a young waitress with a slightly panicked expression.

Now that she was finally here, she could appreciate her surroundings—the fine paintings on the walls, the elegant dimensions of the huge drawing room, which flowed into yet another reception room also filled with people. Vases of flowers, lush and colourful, were scattered on some of the tables, and on the oak sideboard that must have been at least ten-feet long, and the atmosphere was thick with the jollity of lots of people having fun. Young and old, fat and thin, tall and short. She grabbed a glass of white wine from a passing tray and then interrupted Maria, who had been giving instructions on the timing of the food which, she exclaimed, was a complete nightmare to organise—but still, she seemed to be having a great time dealing with her nightmare.

'That dress…' Maria quirked her eyebrows, puzzled.

She was, Cristina acknowledged not for the first time, a strikingly beautiful woman—elegant without being in the least bit intimidating, and well-spoken but gentle with it. Rafael might have been a trifle short-tempered, but she warmed at the memory of him putting himself out on her behalf, showing her up to the room, rummaging amongst his mother's clothes so that he could fetch a selection for her to try on and thereby saving her the embarrassment of greeting strangers with a gaping hole in her dress. And when she had kissed him lightly on his cheek! Her heart did a funny fluttery thing inside her.

She wondered where he was right now. Somewhere in the room, but he had been commandeered by acquaintances long before she had made it over to Maria. Which brought her to the subject of the dress, upon which she launched into an exuberant account of how it was that she was wearing her hostess's dress. Maria, with her head cocked to one side and smiling with amusement, listened to the end and then assured her that she was more than happy for her to keep the dress because it certainly looked a great deal better on Cristina than it ever had on her.

'I've never quite managed to fill it out at the top in the same way,' she confided, instantly boosting Cristina's self-esteem. 'Now, tell me how your parents are…'

They chatted for a few minutes, then Maria took her on a round of introductions to people whose names Cristina had a hard time remembering. By the time Maria disappeared back into the throng, Cristina was happily ensconced in a lively conversation about gardens with some of the locals, who seemed as enthusiastic about the ins and outs of soil and compost as she was.

Across the room, Rafael absentmindedly looked at her and then took himself off in search of his mother, who would doubtless give him a sound lecture on the virtues of punctuality. He wondered how that would favour an early departure from the scene, thanks to an important

overseas conference-call which he had sched-
uled for eleven-thirty.

But no, there was no mention of his late arrival,
and within seconds he knew why.

'I had no choice,' he muttered. 'The woman
had ploughed into the side of the road and was
hunting down an errant contact lens as if she had
a hope in hell of finding it.' He wondered how
well she was taking in her surroundings without
the dreaded spectacles, which she had refused to
wear, opting instead for one contact lens and the
possibility of crashing into something breakable.

She really was generously proportioned in all
the right places, he thought distractedly, finding
her and keeping her in his sight for a few seconds
while he polished off his whisky and soda.

'She's a gem,' Maria said, following his gaze.
'I've known both her parents for such a long
time. They own that chain of jewellers...you
know the ones? Supply diamonds to all the
best people...quietly influential, if you know
what I mean.'

Rafael had been half listening, but now his ears
pricked up, more thanks to his mother's intona-
tion than the substance of her words, though he

was picking up phrases: not brash like most wealthy people… Italian, of course, very traditional in their outlook, but not suffocatingly so… Happy for their youngest to live and work in London… And then, from nowhere, 'She would be perfect for you, Raffy and it's really time you thought of settling down…'

CHAPTER TWO

'NO, MOTHER!'

They were sitting in the large, farmhouse-style kitchen with a pot of coffee between them and the buzz of the radio in the background telling them that another depression was heading in their direction so that they could expect more bad weather.

It was not yet six-thirty, but Rafael had already been up for an hour, travelling the world via his mobile phone and laptop computer, and Maria was up simply because she found it impossible to sleep beyond six in the morning. Waking early was the habit of a lifetime, and a very handy one when she wanted to corner her son before the rest of her overnight guests started drifting down-stairs and commanding her attention.

'You are not getting any younger, Raffy.' She picked at the croissant on her plate and tried to work out a suitable strategy for coaxing him into her way of thinking, a mammoth task by anyone's standards. 'Do you want to grow old changing mistresses every other week?'

'I don't change mistresses every other week!' Rafael informed her. He looked meaningfully at his computer and was dutifully ignored. 'I like my life just the way it is. Moreover, I'm sure she's a very nice girl, but she's not my type.'

'No, I have met your type! All looks and no substance.'

'Mother, that's the way I like them.' He grinned, but met no smiling response. 'I don't want a relationship. I haven't got time for a relationship. Have you any idea how little free time I have in my life?'

'As little as you want to have, Rafael.' She leaned towards him and he could feel a sermon approaching. Mentally he kicked himself for getting downstairs at the crack of dawn when he should have known from past experience that his mother would be there, bustling around and primed for conversation. But he hadn't thought. In fact, he had forgotten her ridiculous remark the minute his conference call had started, just as he had forgotten his brief contact with the girl in question about whom he could only vaguely recall someone short, plump and unnaturally cheerful.

'You can't run away forever, Raffy,' Maria told him in a gentle voice, and his brows snapped together in disapproval of where the conversation was heading. Unfortunately for him, his mother was immune to any such vibes. She just kept ploughing onwards.

'I really don't want to talk about this, Mama.'

'And I think you need to. So you married young and were heartbroken when she died— but, Rafael, it's been over ten years! Helen would not have wanted you to live your life in a vacuum!' Privately, Maria thought that probably was exactly what his ex-wife would have wanted, but she kept the thought to herself, just as she had always kept her opinions of her son's ex-wife to herself. More so now because it was disrespectful to speak ill of the dead.

'For the final time, Mother, I am not living my life in a vacuum! I happen to enjoy my life the way it is!' *And I don't need you to try and find me a suitable wife,* he thought, although he would not have dared utter such a statement because he knew how much it would have hurt her. He was, after all, her only child, and as such a certain amount of interference in his personal life was only to be expected. But that girl of all people? Surely his mother knew him well enough to know that physically the girl just wasn't his type!

She should also have known that any talk of Helen was taboo. That was a part of his life which he had consigned to the past, never to be resuscitated.

Maria shrugged and stood up. 'I should go and change,' she said neutrally. 'People will start heading down in a minute. I wouldn't like to shock them by having to see me in my dressing gown. I am sorry if you think that I'm being an interfering old woman, Rafael, but I worry about you.'

Rafael smiled fondly. 'I don't think you interfering, Mother...'

'The child is a little naive. I know her parents. Is it any wonder that I feel a certain moral obligation that she is okay?'

'She seems fine to me,' Rafael said heartily. 'No complaints about London life. Probably having a whale of a time.'

'Probably.' Maria busied herself with her back to her son, making sure that all the breakfast requirements were ready. Of course Eric and Angela, who had been with her for ever, would have made sure that everything was prepared for her guests—twelve of whom had remained for the night—but she still liked to make sure for herself that all was as it should be. She could hear the guilt in Rafael's voice, but her maternal sense of duty ignored it. She wanted her son to be sorted out, which meant not standing on the sidelines while an array of highly unsuitable women flitted in and out of his life until he eventually keeled over from work-related stress or heart failure.

'Maybe, however, you could make sure that her car is all right for her drive back down to London?' She turned to him for confirmation. 'I told her that you would last night, and she has left her car keys on the table by the front door.'

'Sure.' That small favour seemed more than acceptable when the upside was his mother dropping a conversation that was really beginning to frustrate him.

He would have to do his emails a little later, which was annoying, but unavoidable.

He left the house before further distractions occurred and headed out to where the Mini had been abandoned overnight. Already the sky was beginning to turn the peculiar yellow-grey colour that precedes a snowfall. He realised that if he didn't leave soon he might find himself marooned in his mother's house, subjected to significant conversations about the quality of his life choices.

He was unprepared for the unthinkable, which was a Mini whose engine had decided to hibernate.

An hour after he had left for the seemingly routine task of starting it up, letting it run for a few minutes and then assuring his mother that the car was fine and dandy, he was returning with a ferocious scowl and a premonition of hassle.

He pushed open the front door in a tide of bitterly cold air to find Cristina standing there, warmly clad in jeans and a jumper. The source of all his trouble.

'The thing's dead,' he informed her, slamming the door behind him and stamping his feet on the mat. He divested himself of the beaten leather jacket and glared at her.

Cristina bit her lip, guiltily aware that she should

have been the one seeing to her car, even though Maria had assured her that Rafael wouldn't mind in the least checking on it first thing in the morning. She'd given the impression that it would be no bother at all. From the dark expression on his face, it certainly had been a bother.

'I'm really sorry,' she apologised profusely.' I should have gone and tried myself. In fact, I was about to…'

'Do you think you might have been able to get it going where I failed?'

'No, but…' She fidgeted and then gave him a watery smile. 'Thank you so much for trying anyway. Is it very cold out there? I can make you a cup of hot chocolate, if you like. I'm good at making hot chocolate.'

'No hot chocolate. Black coffee.' He headed towards the kitchen which, thankfully, had not yet been invaded by the leftover guests. As an afterthought, and without turning around to look at her, he offered her a cup.

'I've already had a cup of tea. Thank you.' Cristina paused. Even windswept and scowling he was still rawly, powerfully sexy, just as sexy as he had appeared the night before when he had come to her rescue. She brightened up at the memory of that, the way he had helped her out when there had been no need. 'Do you think I might be able to get in touch with a garage to come and have a look at it?' she asked his averted back.

'It's Sunday and it's going to snow.' Rafael turned around to look at her. 'I think the answer to that is no.'

Cristina paled. 'What am I going to do, in that case? I can't just stay here indefinitely. I've got my job. I can't believe my car's decided to just pack up on me!'

'I doubt it was a deliberate act of sabotage,' Rafael commented dryly, feeling slightly better after the coffee, but still aware that there was a shed-load of work waiting to be done and that he would have to leave sooner rather than later. The motorway would be fine, even if it began to snow, but getting down the lanes that led from his mother's house could be challenging in bad weather, especially in a sportscar which was not fashioned for anything but optimum road conditions.

Cristina smiled and he was dimly aware that she really did have a smile that lit up her face, giving her a fleeting aspect of beauty. However, he was far more aware that time was pressing on, and he looked at his watch and then gulped back the remainder of his coffee.

'I really have to go.' He wondered whether she had any idea of his mother's far-fetched ideas and decided that she didn't.

'I know it's a huge imposition, but could you possibly give me a lift back to London—to whatever Underground station is closest to where you live? It's just that I really need to get back, and…I could always get the garage to come out in the morning and fix the car…and then have someone drive it down to London.'

'Or you could just stay and see to it in the morning yourself. I mean, surely your boss would let you have the day off for an emergency.'

'I don't have a boss,' Cristina said with a touch of pride. 'I work for myself.'

'All the better. You can give yourself a day off.' That sorted, Rafael dumped his cup in the sink and began heading for the door. But the image of her disappointed face behind him made him curse softly under his breath and turn back to her. 'I'm leaving in an hour,' he said abruptly, watching the disappointment fade away like a dark cloud on a sunny day. 'If you're not ready, I'll go without you, because snow's forecast and I can't afford to be trapped here.'

'You could always ask your boss for the day off.' Cristina grinned. 'Unless you are the boss, in which case you can always give yourself the day off.'

But she felt considerably cheered. It was peculiar, but there was something invigorating about him. She packed her bags quickly and efficiently. She hadn't eaten breakfast, but her figure could do with skipping a meal, she decided. And Maria, despite her protests, assured her that she would telephone the garage herself and make sure that the car was delivered to London. She knew Roger, the chap who owned the garage, and he owed her a favour after she had given him a very lucrative tip indeed on the horses.

Rafael was less overjoyed with the arrangements. 'Saddled with' were the two words that sprang into his head. He could hardly blame his mother for the state of the Mini and its lack of co-operation in getting started, but as they manoeuvred down the country lanes one hour later he couldn't help but feel that he had somehow been trapped into sharing his space with a perfect stranger.

And an extremely talkative one who seemed intent on ignoring the fact that he had a handless headset in the car for a reason. She patiently waited for business conversations to end, staring through the window at ominous skies which had gone from yellow-grey to charcoal, and then felt perfectly free to ask him about his work.

'But don't you ever relax?' she asked, appalled after he had reluctantly given her a rundown of his typical day. They were leaving behind the first dismal flurries of snow and Rafael reluctantly abandoned his plans to call his PA, Patricia, for an update on the Roberts deal.

'You sound like my mother,' he told her curtly, then, because he could sense rather than see her baffled silence at the harshness of his response, he relented. After all, he only had a couple more hours in her company. Why be offhand when she was so determinedly upbeat? 'I presume, if you're your own boss, then you know that running a company is a twenty-four-seven commitment. What exactly do you do, anyway?'

Cristina, who had been a little hurt at his lack

of curiosity about her life and what she did, smiled, more than prepared to give him the benefit of the doubt. After all, he was obviously very, very important. She had known, of course, that he came from a moneyed background, but she had had no idea that he was entirely and solely responsible for running the show. Little wonder he was so focused on work with little time to spare making polite chit-chat with her.

'Oh, nothing very important,' Cristina said, suddenly a little abashed at her pedestrian occupation.

'Now I'm curious.' He half smiled, and that half smile made her draw in her breath sharply, made a frisson of awareness ripple down her spine and send shivers racing all through her body. It was scary and exhilarating at the same time.

'Well…do you remember I told you how much I love gardens? And nature?'

Rafael had a dim recollection but he nodded anyway.

'I own a flower shop in London. I mean, it's nothing much. We each of us children came into some money on our twenty-first birthdays and I chose to spend mine on that.'

'In England? Why?' A flower shop? He had had extensive dealings with flower shops, almost exclusively in connection with his girlfriends, to whom flowers were usually sent at the beginning and at the end of relationships. But his PA dealt with all that and he had always assumed that she simply rang one of those huge concerns that delivered worldwide. But there must be one-man-band shows. Cute. She had the appearance of someone who might run a flower shop.

Cristina shrugged and pinkened. 'I fancied being out of Italy. I mean, I have perfect sisters who lead perfect lives. It was nice getting away from the comparisons. But please don't mention that to your mother, just in case it gets back to my parents!'

'I won't,' Rafael promised solemnly. Did she imagine that he gossiped with his mother about such things? Nevertheless, her admission was touching, as was her enthusiasm about what she did. The woman was a walking encyclopaedia on trees and plants, and he was perfectly content to listen as she chatted about her shop, her plans to branch out into the landscaping business at some point, starting with small London gardens, but then moving on to bigger things. She was dying for the Chelsea Flower show, which she had been to a couple of times, and which had never failed to amaze and astound her. Her dream was to show her own flowers there someday.

'I thought your dream was to do some land-scaping,' Rafael said, his cynical palate tickled by her optimistic ambitions.

'I have lots of dreams.' Cristina, aware that she had been babbling, fell silent for a few seconds. 'Don't you?'

'I find it doesn't pay to think too far into the future, which, if I'm not mistaken, is the realm of dreams, so I guess the answer has to be no.' To his surprise, they had reached London quicker than he had expected. She lived in Kensington, not a million miles away from his Chelsea pent-house—and in a rather nice part of Kensington which, he assumed, would have been paid for by those discreetly wealthy parents of hers.

For the first time he considered the advan-tages of a woman to whom his money would be a matter of indifference. His girlfriends were almost always impressed by the size of his bank balance. The ones who did have inherited money were almost worse, in a way, because they were motivated by social standing—playing a game of 'keeping up' or 'going one better' which had invariably involved him being displayed to their other friends as the catch of the day.

This girl seemed to be motivated by neither. Nor, he thought, did she seem interested in playing games with him. There had been none of the usual blatant flirting.

'Seems a bit drastic, moving over here just to escape comparisons with your sisters.'

'Oh, I've been to England hundreds of times. I went to a boarding school in Somerset, you see. Actually, I'm living in my parents' flat, as it happens. And I didn't come just to escape comparisons. Well…actually, I pretty much did. I mean, have you any idea what it feels like to have two gorgeous sisters? No, I guess you don't. Roberta and Frankie are perfect. Perfect in a good way, if you get my meaning.'

'No, I don't.'

'Some people are perfect in a nauseating way, the sort who look glorious and never manage to put a foot wrong—but then they know it and want the world to know it too. But Frankie and Roberta are just lovely and talented and funny and kind.'

'Sound like model citizens,' Rafael said with heavy sarcasm. In his experience such creatures didn't actually exist. He was pretty sure that, like a number of things, they were an urban myth.

'They are, really.' Cristina sighed. 'Model daughters, at any rate. They're both much older than me. I was a bit of a mistake, I think, although my parents would never admit it, and I have to say that I did have a rather wonderful life as the baby of the family. Dad took me to loads of football matches. I think that's why I've always loved football so much. In fact, that's another one of my dreams. I want to do some football coaching. I used to play a lot when I was younger. I was pretty good, in fact, but then I gave it up, and I would really love to get back into it now. Not on the playing level, but on the coaching level. I might put an ad in the papers. What do you think?'

What Rafael thought was that he had never met such a garrulous woman in his life before. He was beginning to feel a little dazed.

'Football,' he said slowly.

'Yes. You know the sport? It's the one that

involves lots of hunky men running around a field kicking a ball…?'

'I know what football is!'

'I was just kidding.' She was beginning to think that here was a man for whom the world was a very serious business.

'You're not exactly a people person, are you?' she mused aloud, and Rafael was stunned enough at that observation to look at her, speechless for the first time in his life.

'Meaning?' he snapped.

'Oh, gosh, I'm sorry,' Cristina apologised. 'I didn't mean to offend you.'

'Why would I be offended by anything you have to say?'

'That's not very nice.'

'It's the truth,' Rafael answered with brutal honesty. He turned down Gloucester Road, slowing to accommodate the pedestrians who seemed to think that crossing roads without watching for oncoming cars was perfectly acceptable Sunday behaviour. Her remark niggled at him and, as he turned right into her road, he slotted his car neatly into a space, switched off the engine and turned to her.

'But I'm curious to find out what you mean by that.'

Cristina reddened and looked at him. 'Oh, just that you don't seem to have much time for fun. I mean…' She frowned slightly. 'Last night, at your mother's party, you didn't seem to be having a good time.'

'Enlighten me.'

'Now you're mad at me, aren't you?'

'Why should I be mad at you?'

'Because even though you say you want me to be honest with you, you don't. Maybe because you're not accustomed to other people telling you exactly what they think.'

'I work in the most cut-throat business in the world. Of course I'm accustomed to people telling me what they think!' Rafael snapped, not really sure how he had ended up having this discussion with her.

'Well, maybe not women, in that case.'

'Maybe I prefer my women to be a little more compliant.'

'Does that mean they've got to agree with everything you say?'

'It helps.'

Cristina thought that it sounded very boring, and since he obviously wasn't a very boring man she wondered how he could tolerate a boring love life—but, before she could expand, he was opening his car door.

'No. Spare me the workings of your mind. I don't think I can take any more refreshingly honest home truths.'

Mortified, Cristina clumsily followed him out of the car and launched into a series of uninvited and unwelcome apologies while Rafael swung her suitcase out of the pocket-sized boot and walked along the pavement to her apartment block.

'Enough!' He held up one autocratic hand and looked at her with frowning impatience. 'There's no need for you to trip over yourself apologising. What's your apartment number? And before you tell me that you can walk yourself and your bag up, I'm escorting you to your door. I may not be a people person, but I do have some rudimentary good manners.'

'Oh, I know you have!' Cristina assured him hurriedly. 'I'm at the top.' She fumbled in her bag for the key, and as she pulled it out he took it from her and pushed open the front door into a flagstone hallway shared by the residents.

It was the sort of place not many young people could ever have dreamed of affording, with the high ceilings and majestic elegance of a converted Georgian building. In fact, it was the sort of place well out of the price range of most people—except, he considered, Cristina was not most people. Underneath the slightly dippy, ready-to-smile, chatty girl lay the soft cushion of family money.

She was walking ahead to the lift, which was small, so small that their bodies were virtually touching when they stepped inside with the overnight bag separating them.

'How long have you been here?' Rafael asked eventually. Somehow prolonged silence in her presence seemed slightly unnatural. He wondered if his brain had somehow gone into overdrive during the long trip back down to London. Could relentless chatter do that to a person?

'You don't have to make polite small talk with me,' Cristina told him, staring straight ahead at the uninspiring view of an elevator button rather than into the mirrored sides of the shaft—which were a little too harsh for her liking when it came to showing up her unprepossessing figure next to his superbly built one.

Even after hours behind the wheel of a car he still managed to look carelessly, breathtakingly, dangerously sexy. She quickly tore her treacherous eyes away from the quick sidelong glance she had given him.

He thought she babbled. Admittedly, she was quite a chatty person. She liked to think of herself as friendly, the sort of person who found it easy to put other people at ease. It was now occurring to her that Rafael might just be the sort of man who didn't particularly want to be put at ease by someone talking constantly at him. He hadn't exactly piled on lots of interested questions, had he? In fact, she had caught him looking longingly at his phone a couple of times, probably, she now thought, because he'd had work to conduct, but politeness had condemned him to silently listen to her whitter on about anything and everything.

'Where did that suddenly come from?' Rafael asked, just as the doors pinged open.

Cristina didn't answer immediately. She hung

back while he opened her door and then breezed past him into her apartment, which was arranged on two floors, the entrance being on the bedroom floor, with a short flight of stairs winding up to the small kitchen and sitting area. It was a tiny apartment, but beautifully proportioned, and interior designers had turned it into a sharply modern unit, kitted out with the best that money could buy. Cristina, who had little interest in the value of things, was unaware of the cost of some of the furnishings surrounding her, many of which had been specially imported from her mother's favourite shops in Italy.

For a few seconds she was tempted to be cool, but being cool did not come naturally to her, and she turned to him and looked up, straight into those amazing blue eyes.

'I just get the feeling that I've been talking too much,' she confessed with her usual directness. 'And if I've been too… too honest with you… then I'm sorry.'

'What makes you think that I don't like your honesty?' Rafael swept aside her apology and started up the stairs. It really was very small, but very, very tastefully done.

'Where are you going?' Cristina called out after him.

'Nice place.' His voice drifted down the stairs and she scurried after him to find him looking around the kitchen, opening her fridge and scrutinising the contents, which were an unhealthy option of pre-cooked meals, cheeses and various items of confectionery which always worked as a pick-me-up when her spirits were a little low.

'You shouldn't be poking around in my fridge,' she announced, slamming the door shut and standing back to look at him. 'I know I don't have the most healthy diet in the world just at the moment...'

Rafael looked down at her. She still hadn't removed her jumper, which was straining across her breasts. Standing there, with her arms folded defensively, she resembled an irate little puppy caught in the act of chewing on a piece of furniture.

'You don't have to defend yourself or your eating habits to me,' he informed her mildly.

'I'm not defending myself,' Cristina lied, blushing madly. 'I'm just...I...'

'Having two saintly, perfect sisters really did

your head in, didn't it?' Rafael really tried not to delve too deeply into the female psyche, but in this instance it seemed impossible to avoid.

'I have no idea what you're on about. I just realise that I could probably do with losing a couple of pounds, and I know what you might be thinking when you nose around my fridge.' She tried to maintain a healthy, dignified silence after this pronouncement, but immediately spoilt it by adding, 'You're thinking that I should be eating lots of salads and drinking lots of mineral water and yes, for your information, I do eat salads.' *Occasionally.* 'Quite often. There.'

'Happy now that you've cleared the air on that count?' Surprisingly, he was amused rather than irritated by her rambling over-explanation. 'A lot of men prefer women who aren't…skinny anyway.'

'Really?' She dredged up some uncharacteristic sarcasm from somewhere. 'Not according to every magazine in every newsagent's up and down the country.' She sighed. 'I was skinny as a child and then I don't know what happened.' She was tempted to open the fridge and dip into some of the cheesecake which she had bought the Friday before for a bit of consolation, but she didn't. That would have really put paid to her futile attempts to convince him that she watched what she ate. And she was dimly aware that she didn't want him thinking the worst of her.

'Anyway,' he said bracingly, 'You're not over-weight. You're curvy.'

Her face broke into a smile of delight and she laughed that infectious laugh of hers. 'Funny, that's exactly what I keep telling myself!'

Rafael looked briefly at her and had a moment of utter madness—a moment when he wanted to touch her, feel her body under the unflattering clothes and find out for himself how curvy she really was, how heavy and succulent those abundant breasts of hers truly were.

He turned away abruptly. 'Fascinating though this is, I'm going to have to leave you. I have work to do.'

'It's Sunday.'

'Try telling that to the rest of the world.' He headed to the stairs while Cristina followed him, unsure whether she would see him again and already telling herself that that was fine. Thoughtful though he had been in sorting her out the evening before, and sexy though he was in a way that sent her entire body into overdrive, there was too much latent aggression inside him, and he was a workaholic. Cristina could respect that fierce work ethic, but she had never found it a particularly attractive trait in a man. The few boyfriends she had had in the past had been kind, unassuming free spirits who, like her, had preferred the great outdoors to the deadly indoors.

That said, she couldn't help but feel a sharp wrench as he opened her front door and turned towards her.

'Thanks for the lift,' she said. 'Of course, I shall send your mother a thank-you note, but if you speak to her please tell her that it was so kind of her to invite me and that I had a marvellous time. I think she's coming down some time next month when my mother comes over to visit.'

She paused for him perhaps to mention bumping into her again, but, deflatingly, he said nothing. He just tilted his head politely to one side, hearing her out, and she wondered whether her rambling gene had kicked in again. 'And don't work so hard.' She smiled. 'Ever so often you should go to the park and have a walk. It's lovely, even in winter.' She very nearly tacked on a lengthy account of what she did when she went to the park—the interesting people she saw, the feeling of peace she got when she sat on a bench and watched the ducks bustling and going about their daily business—but held herself back in the nick of time.

'Thanks for the advice,' Rafael said gravely. 'I'll give it some thought when my working day ends at nine.'

'Now you're laughing at me.'

'Perish the thought.'

He wasn't sure how she had managed it, or maybe it had done him good just escaping London for a night, but he was perfectly relaxed by the time he made it to his own place in Chelsea.

Unlike Cristina, he occupied by London standards an enormous penthouse suite that spanned the top two floors of a redbrick mansion not a million miles away from where she lived. Like hers, his was impeccably decorated, and with a minimalism that left little room for individual touches. Just the way Rafael liked it. No family photos adorned the surfaces, no mementoes of holidays taken, no random books lying dog-eared on tables waiting to be picked up and explored.

Instead, the living area was dominated by two sprawling, cream leather sofas, between which was a thick, cream rug with a barely visible abstract pattern and which had cost the earth.

The paintings on the walls were likewise abstract, splashes of colour which were demanding rather than soothing. Likewise, they too had cost the earth.

He dumped his case on the ground, poured himself a glass of water and immediately went to check his answer machine. Nine messages, eight of which he would deal with later. The ninth…

Rafael played it back with a frown of annoyance.

Delilah. A damned stupid name he had thought at the time, but he had been prepared to overlook that because she was exquisitely beautiful. Very tall, very leggy and with a serenely angelic face that cleverly hid the personality of a shrew.

Theirs had been one of the few relationships which he had allowed to drift, largely because he had been out of the country so much at the time that a face-to-face confrontation had never been engineered, and Rafael had not sought one out. Delilah was prone to hysterics, and if there was one thing that he couldn't stand it was a hysterical woman.

Now, after nearly four months, she was back on the scene. His mother's words slammed back at him—different mistresses every week… running away from a past he never wanted to revisit…living life in a vacuum…

He leaned back on the sofa, closed his eyes and thought that maybe, just maybe, it really was time to think about settling down.

CHAPTER THREE

THAT thought had cleared his mind by the time he awoke on the Monday morning to the insistent beeping of his mobile phone at the ungodly hour of…

Five o'clock!

And a text message from Delilah. The text message, with all those abbreviations which Rafael found so annoying, informed him that she had been away—an extended holiday in the Caribbean—but that now she was back and would love to meet so that they could catch up.

Once a relationship had been terminated, Rafael was the sort of man who moved on. Not for him any scenarios which involved meeting up with an ex-girlfriend so that they could talk over the bad old days about a bottle or two of wine. He had moved on from Delilah, although he had to admit that it had not been a clean break.

Without giving himself time to switch into work mode, he dialled in her number, then waited all of two rings before it was picked up. Not a good sign. Women who waited by phones were women who became very dependent very fast, and a very dependent woman was a liability.

It was not a comfortable conversation and he knew that it should have been conducted face to face. He had optimistically figured that deliberate absence from the scene and a lack of communication would be sufficient indication of a break-up, but he had been lazy.

Hence he could hardly blame her for the tears, the accusations, the insults—which he was unsurprised to hear consisted of a wide range of adjectives—and, worse than all that, the plaintive, rhetorical question of what she had done wrong.

It was nearly six before he was finally off the phone, having endured his full frontal attack, and close to eight by the time he had showered, changed, sent some emails and was heading out of his front door.

It was barely light outside with a cold, blustery wind that felt damp even though there was no sign of rain. Rafael, still in a foul mood after his conversation with Delilah, would have missed the flower shop had it not been open for a delivery just as he happened to be walking past.

He had never noticed it before, but then that was hardly surprising. Flower shops did not feature highly on his list of desired destinations, nor did he often walk to work. It was a vigorous twenty-five minute walk and he could rarely spare the time.

In the bleak mid-winter grey, the scent filled his nostrils and on the spur of the moment he paused then entered the shop.

It was small, but overflowing with flowers, most of which were unusually vibrant, many exotic. One side of the wall was completely given over to orchids, and Rafael was startled at the array. He would have a couple of them delivered to Delilah's house with an appropriate note, but before he could place his order the very young girl who was busying herself with the delivery informed him that the shop wasn't actually open as yet. Not until ten.

'I'll make it worth your while,' Rafael said, glancing at his watch, knowing that he would have to get his skates on if he was to make it to his first meeting. He pulled out his wallet and extracted a wad of notes, then he pointed to the two most exquisite of the orchid plants.

'I want those delivered to this address…' He scribbled Delilah's address on the back of one of his business cards. The young shop assistant was beginning to look flustered, but not for a minute did he think that he wouldn't be able to get what he wanted, because at the end of the day, whether the shop was open or not, money talked.

'I take it there won't be a problem?' He looked up at the girl who glanced over her shoulder and smiled faintly.

'Not at all, sir. What should the message on the card read?'

Rafael frowned and shrugged. 'You're better off without me. All the best. R.' The girl was blushing violently as she transcribed the words onto a piece of paper, and Rafael raised his eyebrows in amusement. 'Would you say that that is appropriate for a relationship that has outstayed its welcome?'

'No! It's horrible!'

Rafael swung round at the voice to find himself staring into a pair of distinctly disapproving eyes, and for a few seconds he was lost for words. Fate had decreed that, of all the small flower-shops he might have walked into from the street on a grainy February morning, he had chosen the one belonging to Cristina.

'Your shop?'

'Anthea, I'll handle it from here.' Cristina, framed in the doorway of her little office at the back of the shop, folded her arms and looked at Rafael, who looked like no businessman she had ever seen before. The uniform was the same— sharp grey suit, just visible underneath the trench-coat which was swinging open, black leather shoes—but somehow he'd transcended 'average man on way to work' into a category of his own.

She turned just as a man approached from the office to stand next to her, and she gave him a bright smile.

'So I can call you later in the week?' she asked.

'Any time after six.'

Rafael watched this brief exchange through narrowed eyes. The man was stocky but muscular, with the build of someone who spent time outdoors. His hair was straight and very fair, and he was wearing an earring which, to

Rafael, immediately spelt 'disreputable'. He scowled and looked around him, waiting for her to finish her conversation.

'Who was that?' he asked as soon as the man had left the shop.

'What on earth are you doing here?'

'What do you think I'm doing? And you haven't answered my question.'

'Anthea…' Cristina was aware of her assistant looking at Rafael, goggle-eyed. 'Why don't you go and start working on the costings for the delivery?

'I know what you're doing here,' Cristina hissed, remembering why she had snapped at him in the first place. 'You're buying flowers, but I'm just amazed that you came here! How did you know the name of my shop? I don't remember telling you.'

'You didn't.' He wondered how her wealthy, no doubt protective, parents would react if they knew that their daughter was in London consorting with all manner of lowlife. 'I happened to be walking to work and I needed to send some flowers to—'

'Someone who had outstayed her welcome?' Cristina, having been raised on a healthy diet of romance fiction and fairy-tale-ending movies, bristled on behalf of the unknown recipient of the most expensive flowers in her shop.

Rafael flushed darkly. 'Had I known that you owned this place, I would have gone elsewhere,' he grated. 'As it stands, you should be grateful that I've just provided some very healthy business for you. I can't imagine that random flower shops do that well in the centre of London.'

'We happen to do very well, as a matter of fact! We specialise in fairly uncommon flowers.' It was not in her nature to be snide, but the devil inside her made her add, 'Maybe guilty businessmen find it works when it comes to buying flowers for their girlfriends. Including the discarded ones.'

'Sarcasm doesn't suit you, Cristina.'

'How could you end a relationship on a note and a bunch of flowers?'

Rafael, unused to being criticised, frowned with displeasure. 'Do you usually leap out of your office and attack people who happen to relay messages you don't like? Isn't that slightly beyond the bounds of good customer service?'

'I couldn't help but overhear,' Cristina

muttered. 'I recognised your voice. You have a very distinctive voice.' She wondered what the mystery woman looked like.

'Can that girl of yours look after the shop for a few minutes?' It would take one phone call to cancel his first meeting and Rafael, who had never cancelled work for any woman, decided that this would just have to be a first. He might have had the girl foisted upon him but, notwithstanding, he had some sense of duty towards her. That included setting her straight on the unscrupulous nature of men in London.

'Why?'

'There's a coffee shop a few minutes away. I passed it on the way here.'

'Aren't you on your way to work?'

'Have you forgotten that I own the company?' No one would guess that, though, Rafael thought with a sense of irony, because he never took time off. In fact, his PA would have to be persuaded not to send round an ambulance crew when he told her that he would be in later than expected.

'I'm going to give you a sermon about how women should be treated,' Cristina felt compelled to tell him, even though the thought of having coffee with him had filled her with a suf-focating sense of excitement. 'Do you still want to take me out for a cup of coffee?'

'Give me five minutes to call my secretary…' As expected, Patricia seemed to hyperventilate when informed that he would have to miss his meeting. Was he really that predictable? he wondered. A man who so consistently put work ahead of everything else that the slightest devia-tion from the norm was enough to bring about heart failure in his employees?

What on earth would they all do if he disap-peared for a week's holiday without warning? Self-implode?

'Okay. Let's get the sermon out of the way.'

'I know I don't have any right to preach to you…'

'No, you don't.' Rafael looked at her over the mug of cappuccino, which she was now attempt-ing to drink even though it was piping hot. A Danish pastry lay on the plate in front of her. In an era of diets and size zeros, it made a refresh-ing change.

Her outfit today was beyond casual, teetering into the realms of the truly bizarre. Workmanlike overalls and a broadly striped jumper which seemed intent on magnifying the generous proportions of its wearer. Since lack of money didn't lie behind her choice, he could only conclude that this was yet another quiet rebellion against those supposedly perfect sisters of hers.

'I don't usually preach to people.'

'Then why break the habit of a lifetime?'

'Why had she outstayed her welcome?' Cristina asked. She carefully rested the mug on its saucer and bit into the Danish pastry, which crumbled on her lips and was absolutely delicious. 'What did she do that was so wrong?'

'Do you live in the real world, Cristina?'

'Why do you say that?'

'She didn't do anything wrong.'

'You just got tired of her?'

'This is what sometimes happens in relationships. People get tired of each other. Delilah was…unsuitable.'

'That's very harsh, Rafael.'

'You have crumbs on your mouth.' He picked up her napkin and brushed them away and Cristina jerked back, startled. 'Don't worry. I'm not about to make a lunge for you.' He laughed, amused at her reaction. 'And I wasn't being harsh,' he continued. 'Delilah and I enjoyed a brief relationship. I never made promises, and it's unfortunate that she didn't understand the boundaries of what we had. Believe me, it wasn't for lack of clarity.'

'How sad.'

'What? What's sad?' Rafael frowned, not caring for the unwanted sympathy in her voice. 'Sad,' he told her, leaning forward, 'Is when two people get together hoping for the fairy-tale ending only to find that no such thing exists. Sad is when hope and expectation disintegrate. If there's no hope and no expectation, then what you get is an uncluttered relationship with no strings attached.' He didn't know why he was bothering to give her a protracted explanation of his theories on the male-female conundrum, especially when her only response was to look at him earnestly as if each word constituted a mound of earth towards the pit which he was digging for himself.

'Have you never been in love?'

Rafael's face tightened. Love? Oh yes. He'd been there, or at least he'd thought he had. In his mind he saw his ex-wife, Helen, beautiful, ethereal, wild with love and promising the earth. How quickly time had dissolved that illusion.

'Have you?' He threw the question back at her and watched her eyes grow dreamy.

'Never. I'm saving myself for the right one. I mean,' she amended hurriedly, 'I don't fling myself into relationships just for the sake of it.'

'What do you mean by saving yourself for the right one?' He raised his eyebrows with rampant cynicism and then mused, with some amusement, 'Don't tell me that you're a virgin…?' Not that he'd believed that for a minute, but from the expression on her face, he realised that he had unwittingly hit the bull's eye, and Rafael was strangely shocked by the thought of that.

'No!' She cast an agonised look around her and then concentrated on the cappuccino in front of her. 'Okay. So what if I am? There's nothing wrong with that!'

He gathered himself and said casually, 'It's just a little unusual…' For a man who never indulged in discussing feelings—which he personally considered the prerogative of namby-pamby men who would rather talk than act—Rafael was surprised to discover that he was enjoying their conversation. It just went to show that a little novelty was good for the soul.

Cristina was horribly, sickeningly mortified by the admission. She had never uttered that confidence to anyone, not to her sisters nor to her friends. To find now that she had uttered it to a man who thought that sleeping around was par for the course was almost beyond belief. The fact that he hadn't roared with laughter only made matters worse, because she could smell his incredulity beneath the silence.

'I realise you must think me a complete loser.' She stuck her chin up, but holding back the tears of embarrassment was an act of will.

'Loser...no.' He leaned forward, both elbows on the narrow table separating them. 'Were you never tempted?' he asked curiously.

'I don't want to talk to you about this,' Cristina whispered. 'Honestly, I don't know how... I've never spoken to anyone about this.' But there was something about this man. A part of her responded to him, and her responses seemed to be totally beyond her control. How was that possible? It was as if he had reached inside of her and tugged at something strong and hitherto unknown, some secret side of her as yet untapped. 'It just slipped out,' she said defensively.

'Your secret's safe with me.'

'I guess you haven't a clue why…well, why…'

'It's a little hard to get my head around.' He had wondered about her, about the feel of her body. Now those meandering and passing thoughts took on a sharp intensity that surprised him. He reminded himself why he had been tempted to take her for a coffee and it was even more relevant now.

'So now we've bared our respective souls…'

'I wouldn't say that you've bared yours.'

'You still haven't told me who that man was, the one closeted in your office with you while your hapless shop assistant was outside taking the flak.'

'Anthea happens to very capable,' Cristina said, temporarily distracted. 'She always handles the business if I'm not around. I've been very lucky to have found her—'

'I can't say I'm overly interested in hearing your shop assistant's CV,' Rafael interrupted, before she headed off down one of those conversational tangents which she seemed so fond of following. 'What I am interested in is the man in the shop. He wasn't there helping with the delivery, was he?'

'Who, Martin? No, no he wasn't.'

Martin? Rafael's ears pricked up. She was already on a first-name basis with the man. She had zero experience of the opposite sex, was a foreigner to the London scene, ignorant of the ways of the average predator—no wonder his mother had been concerned about her and had more or less asked him to keep any eye. No wonder she had seen her as a candidate for the role of wife. Cristina's gentle innocence would have appealed to his mother's traditional heart.

The girl was not just wet behind the ears, she was positively archaic. Whether he liked it or not, she needed some sort of protection, if only from her own naivety.

Rafael decided that he would take on the onerous task of making sure she put into position one or two defence mechanisms which would help her deal with unfortunate situations, such as the one in which she found herself.

'Martin.' Rafael sighed and sat back so that he could study her flushed face. 'Forgive me if I sound like a know-it-all, but I have considerably more experience than you.'

'I realise that.' She was catapulted back into staring at her misguided and very private admission to him a few minutes earlier.

'Which is why I am going to ask you how long you have known this man.'

'Who? Martin?'

'Who else could I possibly be talking about?' Rafael said irritably.

'Well…not very long.' Cristina blushed. 'In fact, he only answered my ad in the local paper last night.'

'You put an ad *in a newspaper*?' Rafael was horrified. His opinion of her as archaic in her approach to the opposite sex was disintegrating rapidly. He wondered how her parents could have merrily waved her off to foreign shores when she was so clearly incapable of holding her own. Maybe they had thought that she needed the experience of standing on her own two feet, but frankly she was like a minnow swimming among sharks. 'Have you any idea how bloody dangerous that can be? Didn't you learn *anything* when you were growing up? How protected *were* you?'

'I don't know what you're implying, Rafael!' Cristina told him defensively.

'I'm implying,' he said in the voice of someone explaining what should have been glaringly self-evident to a halfwit, 'That you should have realised that putting adverts in newspapers in search of the perfect partner is playing with fire. Only two weeks ago there were headlines in the paper about a girl who had travelled to meet a so-called blind date, some lowlife who had answered an advert in a newspaper, only to discover that Prince Charming was actually Ted Bundy. I don't know what this Martin character is like but he looks like a thug. He also wears an earring.'

'I haven't placed an ad—'

'You're inexperienced, Cristina. You're also of a trusting nature. It's a lethal combination.'

'I'm not a complete idiot, Rafael.'

'No, you're not an idiot, and I'm not trying to tell you what to do. I'm just giving you a bit of friendly advice.'

'I don't need your friendly advice!'

Looking at her, Rafael thought differently. The woman was an accident waiting to happen. Even dressed as she was, in that relentlessly unflattering outfit, she still had curves and a figure that a man could want. And something about her face was softly feminine, with those wide, dark eyes and long lashes and a mouth that promised satisfaction. Of course, she had no idea, wrapped up as she was in comparisons to those sisters of hers, comparisons that were cemented in childhood. He wasn't getting through to her, and meeting number one had already been missed. He looked at his watch, and before he could say anything Cristina sprang to her feet, suddenly aware of the passing of time and the fact that there was still an awful lot to do with the delivery of flowers before the shop opened at ten. She also had a relatively large order to dispatch to a hotel for a conference room, and it was a commission which she couldn't possibly ruin because from that could come any number of future orders.

'I have to go,' she said breathlessly.

Rafael, who had been about to say precisely the same thing, wasn't sure that he liked being dismissed. Nor did he care for her heartfelt apology for rushing off because she had some work to do. Wasn't that his prerogative?

'We haven't finished our conversation,' he grated, following her to the door and then along the pavement as she walked briskly back in the direction of her shop.

She turned and flashed him one of those smiles of hers, this time regretful.

'I know, but I didn't like the way the conversation was going anyway.'

'*You didn't like the way the conversation was going anyway?*' Talking to this woman was like taking a magical mystery tour. Rafael had no idea what she would say next and he was beginning to think that, whatever it was, it would be unexpected and not in a pleasant way. Accustomed as he was to women responding to him as a man, Cristina's bluntness was a shock to his system.

'You were practically accusing me of being incompetent in my dealings with other people,' she explained, glancing across at him and feeling that shiver of awareness. 'I know you probably mean well,' she carried on, 'But it's actually a little insulting.'

'Insulting? *Insulting?* Run that by me, because I don't see how I'm insulting you by trying to be helpful! You seem to have forgotten that you were the one who insulted me by implying that I don't treat women well!' He was beginning to feel a little hot under the collar.

'I'm not a simpleton, and if you'd listened to me you'd realise that you'd got it all wrong.'

'Got *what* all wrong?' He wondered if she was about to try and convince him that, with her wealth of inexperience, she knew more than he did about the predatory nature of some men. God save him from ever trying to do a good deed!

'I *haven't* been putting ads in a newspaper for a *blind date*! No one does that these days anyway! At least, not very many. These days people who want to find someone use the Internet!'

'I wouldn't know.'

'I put an ad in the newspaper because I wanted to find out whether there were any opportunities for me to coach a women's football side. Martin replied. He coaches for one of the schools in the area and he thought it might encourage more of the girls to get involved if they had a female coach!'

Rafael grimaced. 'You should have said that from the start,' he admonished.

'You didn't give me the chance!'

They had reached the shop and she turned to him with a little sigh. 'I guess you probably feel some kind of duty towards me because of the connection with our parents,' she said kindly, even though being considered a duty to someone else left a very nasty aftertaste in her mouth. 'But you see, there's no need. I would never, ever try and find my soulmate through a newspaper advertisement!'

'So are you telling me that you've now got a second job working at some school somewhere?' He wondered if she knew how dangerous some schools could be, and immediately reminded himself that she really wasn't his responsibility.

'Not a job, no.' She pushed open the shop door and Rafael followed her in. The delivery of flowers had been sorted out and the shelves were stacked with an extraordinary array of plants, exotic blooms that filled the air with a lush, heavy scent.

Cristina looked at him. 'I've volunteered to coach a couple of classes after school. First one on Tuesday. Martin's not sure what the turnout is going to be, but he's keen to make this work.'

'Where's the school?'

She smiled at him, a sunny smile that lit up her face. 'It's pretty close to here, so I can leave the shop with Anthea and get to the school by five. I'm looking forward to it. I need the exercise, at any rate!'

'Impossible to tell under those layers of clothing.'

She felt his eyes burning through her and the safe, light-hearted change of topic left her feeling heady. 'And you probably need to get back to work,' she reminded him.

'Right.'

He left the scent of flowers, but his mind refused to be reined in by the clinical sanctuary of his plush office. His meetings all went according to plan, but he was distracted and he could feel his PA dithering around him, aware that something was out of kilter.

None of this was going to do. Categorising was his speciality. Women belonged in one category and his work belonged in another, and they never, but never, overlapped. He certainly never found himself staring through his window while his BlackBerry lay on his desk, reminding him that he was contactable twenty-four hours a day without reprieve.

The woman was a liability.

He buzzed through to summon his secretary and on the spur of the moment asked her what his movements were for the next day.

As expected, wall-to-wall meetings, culminating in a mind-deadening event at one of the art galleries. He was surrounded by phenomenally expensive works of art and yet had never actually made it to any of the galleries in the city.

'Cancel everything after four o'clock,' he instructed her. 'I'll keep the art gallery appointment. Some useful people are going to be there.' He had to repeat the request before the blank, incomprehending expression on her face was replaced by her usual efficient one.

But it felt better knowing that he was going to tackle the thorny situation of Cristina and her meeting with a perfect stranger at a strange school. She might be clueless, but he had sufficient savvy for two. Once he had put his mind to rest that everything was as it should be, he would be able to focus instead of having her niggling away at the back of his mind.

And his mother would be pleased. In fact, he was feeling quite pleased with himself later that evening as he poured himself a whisky on the rocks and switched on his home computer, which interfaced with the one at his office, enabling him to take up where he had left off without any glitches.

He might be an unreliable catch when it came to women, he thought, remembering her accusations earlier on—but never let it be said that he was the sort of man who would not do what he could to protect a member of the opposite sex, even if was from herself.

Having established a pleasing moral high ground, he was finally able to devote his usual one-hundred-and-ten-percent to the work at hand, switching off the computer just after it had turned midnight.

And he was in fine fettle by the next day. Altruism, he thought, was certainly an elixir and not just the impersonal altruism of donating to charity. He gave large sums of money to a variety of worthy causes, both through his companies and personally, but he had never felt as invigorated in the process as he did now—knowing that he was doing the right thing and taking someone under his wing.

Someone helpless whether she would ever admit it or not.

When, at four-thirty and just before he was about to leave, Patricia wryly told him that he was almost as scary in a high-spirited mood as he as in a foul one, he actually found it funny and laughed.

'You're laughing,' she said suspiciously. 'You're laughing and leaving work early. Please don't tell me that you've got another Fiona in the background?'

Fiona was one of his exes who had been particularly irritating at the demise of their relationship, and had blown all chances of an amicable parting by bringing her resentment into his work place, much to Patricia's amusement. Patricia, whose contact with his girlfriends was only via the various presents she bought for them and the flowers she sent, had never let him forget 'Fionagate', as she had labelled it. And she had got away with it because she had worked for him for a hundred years and was no longer intimidated by him. She was unique in this.

'Would I be so stupid?' Rafael asked, sticking on his trench coat and making sure that his mobile phone was in his pocket.

'Why not?' Patricia questioned dryly. 'Most men are.'

'Except, of course, for Geoff. Have I ever told you how sorry I feel for that long-suffering husband of yours?'

'Several times. So who is she? Will I be sending her red roses in a month's time?'

Rafael paused. In the space of a few days he had been reminded several times of his relation-ships with women. He had a passing vision of himself as an old man, still chasing beautiful girls for brief affairs. A sad old man. It wasn't a pleasant vision.

'She is a project,' he said slowly.

'A worthwhile one, I hope.'

'That…' Rafael looked at his secretary thoughtfully, '…is something we shall just have to wait and see.'

It was cold and breezy outside and already getting dark. He debated whether to hail a cab, but decided against it. He rarely walked anywhere, mostly because he couldn't spare the time, and the exercise would do him good. He re-membered when he used to play sport. Every sport, excelling in most. Those days seemed to be a lifetime away, before work had become the all-consuming beast it now was.

Before he started indulging in the pointless exercise of reminiscing, Rafael simply refocused on the matter in hand—getting to the school grounds, the name of which Patricia had found out without difficulty, finding Cristina, vetting the Martin character for himself.

Unsurprisingly, the grounds were not located at the school but a bracing fifteen minute walk away. He was pointed in the right direction by a very helpful lady at the school reception desk, and arrived twenty minutes after the football coaching had commenced.

Under the glaring floodlights of the football pitch, he could make her out, surrounded by a meagre assortment of girls who seemed to shuffle about lethargically, while on the side-lines, a large number of boys were making known their thoughts of girls intruding on their territory. The heckling, from a distance, was good-natured, but rowdy, and a couple of the girls drifted away from the pitch to take up ranks with the boys.

Rafael felt a sudden alien surge of protectiveness, but he didn't hurry. Instead, he scoured the pitch for Earring Man, who was noticeably absent.

Then he walked slowly towards the rapidly diminishing group. At this rate, he thought, she would be left with no one to coach, and where the hell was the man who should have been helping her on her first day?

A warm glow of satisfaction spread through him as he felt vindicated in his opinion of the man. Maybe not a thug but definitely a loser.

He was smiling by the time he was within earshot of her. What should have been a coaching session had apparently turned into a coaxing session, but even as she was in the middle of speaking a further two girls, who had been standing at the back kicking the ground in a desultory manner, drifted off to the safety of the group of boys.

She didn't see him at all. In fact, she was only aware of his presence because the jeers on the sidelines had fallen quiet and all eyes were directed to a point just left of her shoulder.

Rafael, skilled in reading an audience, and even more skilled in a sort of a silent but brutally effective intimidation, now called upon both talents.

He flashed a smile at Cristina, who was gaping at him in astonishment, then he looked at the now-mute crowd and simply took control.

CHAPTER FOUR

CRISTINA hadn't known precisely what to expect, but she had been disappointed and taken aback to realise that nothing concrete had been arranged. Martin had made it known during his sports lessons with the kids that they would be initiating a course of football coaching towards getting a girls' team, and had recruited several possibilities, but beyond that he had done very little.

So she had arrived at the school grounds to find her prospective team, but a Martin virtually on the run because his netball team was playing an away game and he had to race halfway across London to get there. He had been full of apologies and had given a pep talk to the girls, while shouting down the boys, and then had disappeared, leaving her in full and complete control of a group of girls inappropriately dressed who seemed to have attended the coaching session out of curiosity and not much else.

Cristina had eyed the glittery trainers and the pink and white track-suits with a sinking heart.

Having never been confronted with a group of young people hell-bent on not listening to a word she had to say, never mind getting themselves dirty on a cold February evening, she had been floundering when Rafael had appeared. Literally like a knight in shining armour. Again. She had almost sagged to her knees in relief.

And he had just…taken over. Cristina had never seen anything like it in her life before. He fought battles in the boardroom, but it appeared that he could also fight on the playing fields, and never mind his sharp suit. He had appeared, sussed the situation, and had immediately been prepared to get his hands dirty so that he could help her!

In an instant, Cristina had forgotten her previous insistence that she didn't require looking after, that she could take care of herself. She had just watched, fascinated, as he'd corralled the girls, who'd been seemingly over-keen to prove themselves on a football pitch never mind the sparkly shoes. Cristina had joined in when the team was in full flow and had taken over. She, unlike the remainder of her team, had dressed very appropriately in clothes that were designed for cold, damp, rain and mud.

An hour later and she had more than her fair share of recruits signing up for the term, and as they left the field Cristina turned to Rafael with a grateful smile.

'You're always rescuing me from tricky situations,' she told him, generous as always in her honesty. 'I don't know what I would have done if you hadn't turned up.' She cast a critical eye at him. 'You're muddy.'

'Next time I'll come better prepared.' Rafael, never having seen himself as the sort of man who went around rescuing damsels in distress, felt quite pleased with himself.

'I'll be fine next time. Really.' They fell into step, leaving the grounds behind him.

'Where was the Martin character?'

'Oh, he introduced me to the girls, but then he had to rush off for a netball match. Not his fault.'

'You're too generous,' Rafael said shortly. 'The very least the man could have done was to stick around and show you the ropes on your first day.'

'I know,' Cristina said vaguely. 'But his match had been arranged a long time before he knew that I would be coming here. I'm just happy that he gave me the chance to do this.'

Rafael frowned, not caring for the way she immediately rushed into the man's defence.

'You'll be royally taken advantage of with an attitude like that,' he told her darkly, and he felt her briefly touch his arm.

'You're far too cynical, Rafael. Why would Martin take advantage of me? I'm volunteering to do this! It's hardly as though he's going to rope me in to do all manner of school activities. He knows I've got a full-time job with the flower shop.'

'You can never tell. You're far too trusting.'

'Well, that's not such a bad thing, is it?'

Rafael laughed dryly. 'I wouldn't know. It's not a trait I'm familiar with. In the cut-throat world of business, having a trusting nature is like loading a gun and pointing the barrel at your head.'

Cristina shuddered. 'Which is why I will never get involved in that world.'

'No. I can't say I can see you there.' Rafael, imagining her sitting in a board room discussing mergers and acquisitions, couldn't resist a smile. It felt surprisingly good to be walking along the busy London streets with his shoes muddy, his suit fit for the bin and his trench coat whipping around him. 'There's no point my going back to the office,' he told her suddenly. 'I'll take you out to dinner.'

'You don't have to do that.'

'I realise that.' He stuck out his hand and magically a taxi appeared. He pulled open the door, gave the cab driver her address and turned to her. 'Well?'

'Yes!' Cristina said breathlessly.

This wasn't any kind of date. She knew that. Rafael was not the sort of man to be attracted to her. But still…it felt like a date and she showered quickly and dressed accordingly, making it casual, but as sexy as she could given the restrictions of her figure. Instead of her usual over-sized jumper, she wore a tightly fitted knitted long-sleeved top in a pale apricot colour. The jeans remained the same but with boots, and she finger-brushed her hair and left it loose.

It took her less than forty-five minutes from start to finish and her eyes were bright when she rejoined him in the kitchen, where he had helped himself to some water while he waited.

She looked good.

Rafael gazed at her in astonishment because the figure only briefly glimpsed before now revealed itself as curvaceous and ultra-feminine. A tantalising strip of cleavage pouted provocatively at him from between the folds of her coat.

Sweet natured, naive and from the right background. She would never demand anything, and would never see him as a bank balance in need of depleting. If there was one thing he had established beyond a shadow of a doubt, it was that she was uninterested in money. She had plenty at her disposal, thanks to her parents, and yet no one would ever have guessed it. He continued to look at her speculatively until she began to squirm under his scrutiny.

'What?' she laughed nervously. 'Have I got something on my face?'

'You look good.' This was the first time Rafael had ever contemplated approaching a relationship with longevity in mind. At least, the first time since his disastrous marriage all those years ago. Then, he had made a terrible mistake. It had been a vital learning curve, and Rafael had no intention of repeating his error. He had never allowed his mother to dictate his love life, but this time he was prepared to allow that time was marching on. The vision of a lonely old man had spread before him in all its dubious glory and he hadn't cared for it.

This woman fitted the bill of a suitable wife. The icing on the cake was that the union would be given full approval by his mother, who had uniformly disliked every single woman he had ever brought to see her, and that, he had always known, included his ex-wife.

'Thank you.' Cristina went bright red and reminded herself that this was not a date. Like he had said, neither of them could have really returned to work, and he'd probably had nothing better planned for the evening.

'Now to my place so that I can shower, and then we could head off. What kind of food do you like?'

'All kinds!' She chattered happily as they jumped into another taxi for the twenty-minute trip to his apartment. She confessed to having a sweet tooth, filled him in on the numerous diets she had sampled over the years, talked about what she wanted to do to her football side, and then anxiously asked him whether he thought it was a good idea or not.

She was simple and uncomplicated and he knew, instinctively, that she would not put him in the pressurised situation of having to dismiss her because she had overstepped her brief.

'Did you mean what you said about coming back for another go at the football?' she asked suddenly. 'You told me that the next time you would be better prepared.'

Rafael had enjoyed the game. He had not really played, just stood on the sidelines giving her a hand, but now he thought that maybe he would make the time. He had played both rugby and football all the way through school and university and had excelled at both. However, along with most other leisure activities, he had promptly dropped both the minute his working life had taken over. Now, perhaps, he would redress the balance.

He nodded slowly and looked across at her expectant face. 'Why not? I can arrange to come along at least now and again, especially if your so-called buddy is going to do another runner.'

It felt good to be accommodating, and he knew that his efforts would be worth it. He would court her the good old-fashioned way. Marriage as a business proposition would not be her style, and he wouldn't blame her. But it certainly would work for him. Love was a complication, and after years of unforeseen complications in his dealings with women he was ready to concede that what he needed was a marriage of convenience.

'Really?'

'You sound shocked.' He gave her a half smile that made her pulses race.

'I am,' Cristina told him truthfully. 'I got the impression that you didn't make time in your life for very many leisure activities, least of all football with a bunch of high-school kids.'

'I'll have you know that I was a pretty impressive player in my time.'

'What happened?'

'Work happened.'

'Well, it's never too late to loosen those chains,' Cristina said gently.

'Chains?'

'The ones that are keeping you tied to your desk.'

They had reached their destination. Was it her

imagination or were they beginning, against all odds, to bond? She could scarcely believe it. He was utterly out of her league, at least in terms of physical attraction and social *savoir faire*. She, like him, came from a privileged background, but there the similarity ended. And yet she could feel something tentative between them. It was scary and exhilarating at the same time, and it made her head spin, as if she was twelve again and on one of those terrifying rollercoaster rides she had gone on with her friends.

Having no experience on which to fall back, Cristina contented herself with some pleasurable fantasies in which Rafael played the starring role.

When he emerged, dressed, they had already had two children and a couple of dogs.

She flushed guiltily, relieved that he couldn't read her mind.

They went to a Thai restaurant, and it was only when they were nearly through a bottle of wine that Rafael asked her casually how it was that she had never had a boyfriend.

'Of course I've had boyfriends!' Cristina told him hotly. 'I just never met anyone I wanted to settle down with.'

'And that would be because…?'

'I must be fussy,' she responded airily, pleasantly heady after the wine.

'Oh, yes?' Rafael leaned forward. Her cheeks were pink, her eyes bright. She wasn't flirting with him, but there was something undeniably sexy about her—they way her lips were parted, the way her heavy breasts bounced when she gesticulated, which she did a lot. He reached out, forked one of the prawns on her plate and placed it to her mouth.

Cristina went a brighter shade of pink and nibbled the proffered delicacy. Such a small gesture, but it sent her pulses racing and made the hairs on the back of her neck tingle.

'You're blushing,' he said, flirting outrageously but keeping his expression perfectly serious. 'Why? Do I make you nervous?'

'A little, I suppose,' she confessed. 'Can I ask you something?'

'Anything you like.' Rafael sat back, sipped his wine and watched her carefully over the rim of his glass.

'Are you flirting with me?'

'I beg your pardon?'

'Are you flirting with me?'

Rafael, taken aback by the directness of the question, was stumped for words. 'What if I were?' He finally answered her question with one of his own.

'I would ask you why.'

This was not a conversation Rafael had ever conducted with a woman before, but then he had to concede that this woman was not exactly like any woman he had ever dated before. Next she would be asking him if this, in fact, was a date, and if so could he please give her his definition of a date!

'Well?' It took some courage, but Cristina was determined to find out where exactly she stood. There would be nothing more mortifying than to conduct herself in a manner that suggested she wanted more from him than he was prepared to give. He was a man of the world. The last thing he needed was to lend a helping hand only to find the subject of his noble attentions was becoming a nuisance.

'If it's flirting when I tell you that you look sexy, then I'm flirting.' The roundabout approach was, he was finding, strangely enjoyable. Something of a turn-on, in fact.

'Sexy? Me?'

Rafael leant towards her, his face still serious. 'I'm a connoisseur of women and you have a very delectable body, Cristina.'

'I'm…I'm not sure that I approve of…of having my body looked at…in that way…' she stuttered, swallowing a deep breath. 'I've never appreciated men who—who treat women like objects.'

'And I apologise if that was the impression I gave you.' Their food was placed in front of them, lots of little taster dishes, with the delicious aroma of coconut and peanut.

Cristina stared down at the fragrant selection, dismayed to find that, although she had been sticking up for her principles, she wished that she hadn't wrecked the atmosphere in the process. And why kid herself? She had liked his remark. It had been out of order, but she liked that he had been looking at her body. Her mind had gone into overdrive and she had pictured him touching her. Just thinking about it now made her feel hot and bothered.

'Okay.' She smiled shyly at him. That was her way of flirting. She thought it might have been more coy if she hadn't gone bright red, but she was new to this game.

Rafael, smiling lazily back at her, knew that he was winning, and a very pleasant game it was turning out to be too. Not for a moment did he think that he was being unfair, that he was using his tremendous and powerful appeal to sneak under her skin and break down her defences. Indeed, he thought that he was doing her a favour in not sitting her down and discussing with her, rationally and thoughtfully, the pros and cons of marriage as a business transaction. If that wasn't respect for her values, then what was?

He raised his glass to her in an indolent toast and kept his fabulous eyes pinned to her face as they sipped their wine.

'Do you know?' Cristina confided as she finally closed her knife and fork on what had been a superb meal. 'I feel as though I've known you for ages. Isn't it weird?'

'Wcird,' Rafael agreed. She was as transparent, he mused, as a pane of glass. There was no teasing 'getting to know you, getting to know me' game, no suggestive remarks designed to get his appetite whetted, no come-hither looks to pique his curiosity.

'Except,' she frowned, 'I don't really, do I?' She

linked her fingers together and stared at him, thrilling at the sheer beauty of his face, his sensational sexual allure. He was flirting with her, teasing her, and although she didn't know why, because he could have snapped his fingers and had any woman he wanted on the face of the planet, she was happy to just accept the situation as it presented itself to her. She wasn't someone who spent a lot of time analysing things. What good did that ever do? Growing up, she had had friends who'd analysed relationships into an early grave, and she had learnt that trying to read too much into things was usually a cause of unnecessary stress. Aside from that, her sunny personality was not given to brooding on possibilities.

Something about this man—and she knew it went way beyond the fact that he was stunningly, shockingly beautiful—went straight through her sexual reserve and struck at the very core of her.

'How well do we ever know someone else?' Rafael was amused by the ease she felt in his company. He wasn't a fool. Even when women had been chasing him, even when they had been lying in bed with him, he had known that they had tiptoed around him, as though apprehensive that the man who made love to them could suddenly turn into a monster.

'That's a silly answer,' Cristina said bluntly, and Rafael burst into laughter, highly amused at her response.

'A silly answer… Nooo…'

'No what?'

'Nope. I've searched through my memory bank and I can't recall anybody ever telling me that something I've said is silly.'

'You're making fun of me.'

'Perish the thought!' He ordered them both coffee and then sat back, relaxed, to hear where she would go from here. Surprisingly, they had managed to consume between them the better part of two bottles of very fine white wine indeed. Italian, naturally.

'It's just that you pretty much know everything about me. I've told you about my family, my sisters, my schooling, my flower shop. But you haven't told me anything about yourself. I know you work hard and do something clever in business, but what else?'

Rafael thought of the never-ending hours of

work he put in running companies that stretched across the world, and was amused to have it all reduced to doing 'something clever in business'.

'Went to school, did economics, physics and psychology at university, left with a first-class degree…'

'You did psychology? Frankie wanted to do psychology at university, but dad told her that it was a soft option so she did history instead. As it turned out, she never actually used her degree cos she got married and had children. I guess you find it useful in business, though—you can interview people and know exactly what they're really thinking.'

'Psychology, Cristina,' Rafael said dryly, 'As opposed to mind-reading.' He fell silent for a few seconds and then made a decision. 'And, yes, I guess it is useful in business. Knowing how people tend to think gives you a headstart on figuring out their moves, which can come in handy when you're sitting round a table trying to hammer something out. Aside from that, it's been less effective than you might think.'

'What do you mean?' She was hardly aware that she had finished her coffee and was watching him intently, sensing that he was on the brink of a revelation of some kind. Was she holding her breath? She forced herself to breathe evenly because this was really no big deal. He was probably on the brink of disclosing something really trivial, like he hated cooking or didn't know how to use his washing machine, or had cried when his pet rabbit had died when he was a kid.

'I was married once…' Rafael gave her a crooked smile. He had decided to embark on this topic because his marriage was no secret, and sooner or later she would find out about Helen from his mother. He wanted to set the record straight from the start. However, now that the words had left his mouth, he discovered that confiding was a talent he lacked, never having put it to any use.

'You don't have to go into any details,' Cristina said hurriedly, partly because she could sense his difficulty in talking about it and partly because, in this little fantasy world she was busily spinning for herself, hearing about a woman who could turn out to have been the love of his life was not what she wanted. 'I mean,' she continued quickly, 'I know men aren't very good at expressing their feelings…' She had read that somewhere and in her limited experience it was certainly true. 'Well, obviously some men are,' she ploughed on for the sake of accuracy.

Rafael experienced one of those moments of slight disorientation that conversing with her seemed to generate.

'Some men can be very sensitive.' She frowned earnestly. 'Of course.'

'Of course,' he agreed blandly, once more back in control. 'Men who cry in front of sad movies and think that knitting shouldn't be a sexist thing.'

This time it was Cristina's turn to laugh, which drew a smile from Rafael.

'I got married to a woman called Helen when I was… Well, put it this way, young enough to be fooled into thinking that it was love.'

'And it wasn't?' Cristina asked hopefully.

'It was a catastrophe.' This was the real version of events and one he had told no one, not even his mother. This was the version of events which he had had no intention of telling her, but somehow his brain had failed to transmit that message to his mouth—and here he was, recounting a story that was older than time, but that still filled him with sour bile whenever he thought about it. Which was seldom.

He would keep it brief, he decided. 'We met at university,' he said in a clipped, impersonal voice. 'At one of those clubs where too much beer gets drunk and everyone rolls back to halls of residence way too late, stopping for a curry on the way back.'

Cristina tried to imagine a wild and reckless Rafael, drunk and eating a curry, and found that she couldn't.

'Helen was there. Unlike everyone else, she was stone-cold sober, just standing a little apart from her group, looking around her.' Rafael remembered that look. It had been cool and detached, as if she'd been examining the crowd and had possibly found it wanting, and it was that look that had drawn his attention. The look and her amazing beauty: hair platinum-blonde, body tall and languid, eyes of a most incredible green. He had wanted her the minute he had laid eyes on her and, even at the age of twenty, had known that he would have her.

He heard himself explaining that moment to his rapt audience, the moment he had felt something way beyond anything he had ever felt before. Had continued feeling it, like a man in a trance, even when little snippets of information had emerged that should have had the alarm-bells ringing.

'She was older than me, as it turned out,' he said dispassionately. 'A little something she kept to herself, and the fact is I probably would never have been the wiser if I hadn't come across her passport buried in one of her drawers. Nine years older, to be precise. Nor was she a university student. She actually worked at a department store in the city.' He shook his head, and although he couldn't detect the bitterness in his own voice Cristina had no trouble in hearing it, and her tender heart reached out to him.

'We married as soon as I was out of university, by which time she naturally was well aware of the extent of my personal fortune. My ex-wife,' he said heavily, 'Was instrumental in showing me the truth behind the saying that all that glitters is not gold. It wasn't long before I realised that she was long on good looks, but pretty short on fidelity.'

'How awful for you,' Cristina said softly, which

reminded Rafael that he was in the process of pouring his heart out, a self-indulgent exercise for which he had no taste. But she made a good listener, and it felt oddly liberating to talk to her.

'To cut a long story short…' He signalled for the bill and briefly scanned it before handing over his credit card. 'It wasn't long before she began casting her net elsewhere, while continuing to enjoy the sort of lavish lifestyle she must have been quietly searching out all her life. She was involved in a fatal car crash in America, and only I am aware of the fact that she wasn't the driver of the car. I believe he was the ski instructor she had met the year before.'

'That's just awful,' Cristina said softly and, far from being irritated by a clichéd response, Rafael was touched by the depth of feeling in her voice.

'That's just…life. So, now you have been treated to a slice of my past, it's time for us to head home. You have work tomorrow and I have a do later tonight which, I might add, I am already late for.' He stood up, surprised at the speed with which the evening had progressed.

'Won't they be a little put out? It's after nine!'

'It's not the sort of affair that requires strict adherence to time,' Rafael said, thinking without vanity that he would be welcomed whatever time he decided to appear because they had more need of him than he had of them. 'But…' Yet another uncharacteristic decision. 'You are right. The thought of walking around an art gallery and trying to look interested in splashes of random colour on a canvas might be a bit of a struggle at this hour.' He quickly made a couple of calls, and by the time he had clicked off his mobile his appearance at the gallery had been cancelled.

It was beginning to rain outside, an icy rain that spiked their faces like thin needles. Against this penetrating cold Cristina's coat was defenceless and she was glad to step into a taxi and sit back, eyes closed as she rehashed in her mind her extraordinary afternoon and evening. The football coaching had started off with such lack of promise, and had ended in her sharing a meal with a man to whom she was—and she didn't mind admitting it—strangely and intoxicatingly attracted. A man who was attracted to her!

He had confided in her. Had that been a turning point for him?

'You're not going to fall asleep on me, are you?' Rafael asked as he heard her try to stifle a yawn.

'Sorry.' She shifted in her seat and looked at him drowsily. 'Must be all that wine after running around coaching. I feel exhausted.'

Rafael started to say something and then noticed that her eyelids were drooping. It dawned on him that she was nodding off in his company. Was this what they meant by sending someone to sleep?

By the time the taxi was outside her apartment, she was leaning against him, breathing evenly, sweetly asleep. Her hair smelled fresh and clean. He gently nudged her, and Cristina woke with a little start and straightened up, apologising profusely for falling asleep.

Her eyes were still drowsy. She looked like a little rumpled puppy.

'I'll see you in, and before you tell me that I don't need to I know I don't. But I will anyway.'

'Am I that predictable?' she asked, waking up more fully as she stepped out into the rain.

'No,' he drawled slowly. 'Predictable isn't a word that could be used to describe you.'

It was only when they were in the lift that

Cristina, fully alert now, became aware of the atmosphere between them. Something had changed, although she couldn't precisely say what. They both knew something about each other that was unique to them. She knew about a slice of his past which he had shared with no one else, and he knew that she was a virgin, and this intimacy seemed to have altered something. Altered it in a thrilling and very charged way. She kept her eyes studiously averted in the lift, but every nerve in her body was aware of him standing next to her, his hair damp from the rain, his hands thrust into the pockets of his trench coat.

The lift doors purred open and, like a bolt from the blue, Cristina realised what had been lying at the back of her mind ever since she had set eyes on Rafael, ever since he had come to her rescue at his mother's party.

For reasons quite beyond her, he had awakened something in her, a sexual side that had been in hiding, waiting for the right moment. Even though he wasn't the right man, he still did things to her, made her feel alive, sent all her senses on red-hot alert.

And she couldn't help but think that he felt

something for her as well. Everything pointed in that direction because, really and truly, why would he pretend an attraction that wasn't there? What would be the point?

Never in her wildest imagination had she ever thought that he might really find her sexy, but it seemed that he did—and the realisation was as powerful as a drug, firing her blood, making her giddy with excitement.

Her hands were trembling as she inserted the key into her door and let them both in to her apartment.

This time she didn't, as she might normally have, turn to him with a polite, friendly smile, thank him for the lovely meal and wait for him to leave as she stood sentinel by her front door. This time, she just half turned and asked him whether he might care for a cup of coffee.

She shrugged off her coat, hung it over the banister and without giving him time to frame an answer headed up the narrow stairs, her heart beating so loudly that she swore that, had there been complete silence, she would have heard it over the patter of the rain outside.

As it was, she could hear him following up the stairs, and when he was standing framed in the doorway of the small kitchen she was already fetching two mugs down from the cupboard.

He had disposed of his trench coat and of the beige cashmere jumper and had rolled the sleeves of his shirt to the elbows.

'I know.' She thought her voice sounded jumpy and she cleared her throat. 'It's really warm in the flat. I can't bear to be cold inside, so the heating's always turned up.' She gave a nervous little giggle. 'I can't imagine what I'm doing for the global warming situation. You know, you see these adverts on telly: carbon footprints…should wash clothes at thirty degrees instead of forty…' She was talking too much. She blushed and stared down in a fixated fashion at the coffee which she was now spooning into the mugs.

In the silence, her eyes skittered across to him. He hadn't moved from his position by the door, although he was now leaning against the door frame and smiling at her.

'Would you believe me if I told you that I'd never met anyone like you before?' he asked lazily.

'Would you say that that's a compliment?'

'Isn't it always a compliment to be told that you're unique?' he said, and for a few seconds

Cristina thought that he hadn't exactly answered her question, at least not in a very satisfactory way. But her thoughts scattered at his expressive, glinting smile. It transfixed her and brought all coherent thought skidding to an abrupt stop.

Rafael walked towards her and rescued the kettle from her shaking hands, then he poured boiling water into the mugs.

'There you go again,' he murmured softly. 'Acting like a cat on a hot tin roof. Are you nervous because I flirted with you over dinner?'

Cristina, lost in the depths of those fabulous blue eyes, shook her head dumbly. It was impossible to think straight when she was looking at him, when he was looking at *her,* like that. It was as if time had stood still, and in that moment everything seemed heightened: every sense, every noise, the faintest flutter of her heart.

Her hand reached up and she soundlessly stroked the side of his face, tracing the harsh, beautiful contour of his cheekbone. And then, standing on tiptoe, her eyes closing as she neared him, she softly covered his mouth with hers.

CHAPTER FIVE

RAFAEL didn't know whether it was the hesitancy of the gesture or the implication behind it, but the result was explosive. One minute he was coolly playing with the notion that this woman, unexpectedly, might very well be the one who made sense when it came to settling down…and the next minute his body was reacting to a simple touch as if she were the first woman to have laid hands on him.

He didn't stop to question his reaction.

Coffee was forgotten as he returned that tentative kiss with one of his own. He curled his fingers into her hair, tilting her head back so that he could plunder her sweet, eager mouth with his tongue, until her body curved against his. He could almost feel her heartbeat, and when eventually they surfaced for oxygen he held her back, breathing thickly,

'Are you sure you want this?' he questioned unevenly. Never before had he asked a woman whether she wanted to sleep with him. In that game called love—or rather, as far as he was concerned, *lust*—the rules were perfectly understood. It had always been a ritual, a courtship routine, the only difference being that the routine had never led to permanence.

How ironic that he should now give this woman the chance to back out when she was the chosen one.

He would also not be making the inevitable speech about not getting involved, about enjoyment without strings. He was filled with a strange sense of liberation. Also, the realisation that his mother had been right, that he had reached an age to settle down—and he counted himself fortunate that he was mature enough to view the situation in a cool-headed manner, to work out the most appropriate partner, thereby eliminating the possibility of failure. It was comforting to know that he could rationalise a relationship in the same way that he could rationalise a spreadsheet.

He wished that he had had that knowledge at his

disposal all those years ago when he had leapt into marriage because of that non-existent, illusory and ludicrously overrated misconception called *love*. He wished that someone had told him then what he knew now, which was that there was no such thing as love. There was common sense, and that, above all else, was the lubrication that kept the wheels of a relationship turning.

Cristina looked at him with absolute conviction and nodded. She couldn't help but be impressed by the fact that he hadn't just taken what had been on offer, but had given her the opportunity to change her mind had she so wanted. How many men would have done that?

She half closed her eyes and this time, when his mouth touched hers, it was with devastating tenderness. She wrapped her arms around his neck and moaned very softly as he trailed kisses over her fluttering eyelids and damp cheeks before recapturing her mouth.

'I think we should continue this in the bedroom, don't you?' he asked softly and Cristina sighed in wordless agreement.

Once there, she stared at him in open fascination as he began removing his clothes, and when he looked at her with wry amusement she blushed, but didn't look away, and nor did he seem in the slightest bit bothered by her absorption.

Only when he was down to his boxer shorts did her nerves begin to kick in and she was overcome with sudden, horrendous shyness.

'Don't worry,' Rafael murmured, oddly touched by the nervous, wary expression on her face. He walked slowly towards her, not wanting to frighten her. He was massively and unashamedly turned on, could feel his erection pushing up against the boxers, but he was going to take his time.

'I'm not worried.' Cristina chewed her lip, dragging her eyes away from that bulge, which was both a heady turn-on and a source of fear. 'Okay, I *am*. Just a bit. I'm not…I don't know…'

'I'll take care of you,' Rafael said gently.

Cristina nodded gratefully, and continued staring at him, at his powerful, masculine beauty—the broad, brown shoulders, the narrow, tapering waist, the latent strength in his body that was visible every time he moved. There was something so graceful about him even though he was so impressively built. He was so much more experienced than she was, had had so many lovers. That was a little scary, as was the knowledge that all those lovers would have been as physically perfect as he himself was.

Cristina determined to put that out of her mind and focus instead on the extraordinary and exhilarating fact that he found *her* attractive.

'I've never actually undressed in front of a man before,' she confessed.

'And it turns me on to think that I'm the first,' Rafael told her truthfully. He would have liked to place her hand firmly on his erection, have her feel him, but he knew that he would have to wait for that, and he was happy to do that. He began undressing her and, as eventually skin touched skin, he was aware of her trembling apprehension.

Through the window, the ever-present London night-light filtered through so that they weren't in pitch blackness.

He curved his hands to cup her breasts, which were still in the lacy bra that, in the half light, was like a tattoo on her skin. He knew that his breathing was unsteady, his body violently aroused by the lingering disrobing. Rafael had to steel himself against rushing, but it was damned hard taking his time, tracing a lazy outline of her breasts, when he wanted to rip aside that thin barrier of fabric so that he could lose himself in what they so barely contained.

His taste in women had been formed from habit: leggy, rake-thin, exquisite clothes-horses with no spare flesh. They had looked good and had turned heads, but they had not felt like this. This woman's body proclaimed her femininity, with all its curves and abundance. He ran his hands along her sides where her waist dipped in, giving her an exquisite hour-glass shape, and felt the waistband of her matching underwear. He slowly slipped his fingers under the elasticated waistband and felt her indrawn breath.

He knew that she would be wet for him, but instead he removed his hand and began to gently unclasp her bra, murmuring soothing noises into her ear.

The sight of her naked breasts filled him with a savage adrenaline rush. He couldn't stop a groan of pure pleasure from escaping him as he cupped them and began massaging them, rolling his thumbs over her stiffened nipples, taking it very slowly until her rapid breathing slowed to low whimpers of satisfaction.

By the time he edged her towards the bed, she was more than ready for the feel of his mouth as it covered one of those tempting circles.

Cristina had been saving herself all her life for this, and it was glorious. She gazed down at his dark head nuzzling her breast and writhed, now closing her eyes, at the sharp, delicious sensations evoked by the feel of his mouth and tongue working against the sensitive bud. Her entire body was aflame with a weird, wonderful, exquisite pleasure that made her want more. She arched up and wriggled instinctively against that exploring mouth, guiltily ashamed of this unforeseen wanton side that was suddenly and shatteringly released.

She was desperate to rip off her briefs, unable to contain her own body's response to his caresses.

As he left her breasts to trail hot kisses along her stomach, Cristina sat up and pulled him up to her. 'What are you doing?' she squeaked and he grinned with boyish charm.

'Relax. I won't be doing anything you won't enjoy.'

Cristina wondered how she could possibly relax when he was about to touch her *there*, her most intimate place, with his mouth. She was unprepared for her electrifying response as he parted those delicate folds and began caressing her with his tongue. The glory of what she was feeling stopped all her incipient inhibitions dead in their tracks, and she began moaning as he continued to lick that wildly sensitised nub until she could feel her own inevitable climax approaching.

No! Even in her innocence, she knew that lovemaking should be a two-way process, and she limply tried to struggle up, but her efforts were useless against the inroads he was making with his expert lathering. She dropped back against the pillows, unable to do anything but watch his head moving between her thighs, and then she was lost in wave upon wave of shameless pleasure which had her arching back, crying out at the intensity of her fulfilment.

'I'm sorry,' she whispered, mortified at her lack of control over her own body.

Rafael, still recovering from the intensity of

satisfaction he had derived from pleasuring her, gave her a bemused look. 'You're sorry?' It dawned on him that regrets were beginning to sink in with her. She had been swept away on those notoriously unreliable wings of temptation and now she was fast recovering her senses. 'Sorry about what?' He levered himself up so that he was alongside her and, once there, he had to make use of all the will power at his disposal not to touch those breasts, which could drive a man wild with desire.

'It…it shouldn't have happened like this…' Cristina whispered, truly devastated that a man of his experience had been doomed to end up with a partner like her, someone utterly clueless between the sheets. She could feel the onset of tears forming at the back of her throat, and she swallowed them down shakily.

'Like…what? Do you regret what's just happened between us?' As confident in the bedroom as he was in the board room, Rafael now felt himself floundering in unmarked territory.

'I don't regret it,' Cristina said miserably. 'But…but I… It can't have been very satisfying for you…'

Rafael almost laughed but he contained himself, suspecting that she might interpret such a response in the wrong light. Instead, he stroked the side of her cheek and smiled.

'I have no idea what you're talking about,' he told her gently, which induced another watery smile.

'I've read articles. Men like to be satisfied through full intercourse...if they aren't...' Cristina tried to remember what happened if they weren't. 'Doesn't that lead to dangerous blockages? Or something...?'

Rafael felt his lips twitch and he cleared his throat noisily. 'That's not a consequence I've ever heard of before,' he said seriously. 'And I happen to be completely satisfied.' He leaned forward and kissed her very gently on the lips. 'Believe me when I tell you that your response to being touched was immensely gratifying, and I feel privileged to have...given you pleasure.'

Cristina felt the sun burst through the clouds and this time her smile was full of shy warmth. He was a generous lover. Had she really expected him to be otherwise? Hadn't she known, somewhere deep inside, that that would be the case? Hadn't she known that this man, however wrong he might seem on paper, and however vastly different their levels of experience were, was right in every sense of the word?

Fate, she now thought, had seen fit to throw them together for a reason, and the reason was *this*.

She took his hand and placed it on her breast, and she loved as he drew in his breath sharply, as if in the grip of something over which he had no control. When he guided her hand to him, it was completely natural and when, after a blissful and leisurely foreplay, they made love, it was glorious. Wonderful. If she could have made time stand still, she would have done so. She would have liked to bottle the memory and kept it close to her for ever, so that she could breathe it in whenever she wanted.

'What are you thinking?' Rafael asked, propping himself up on one elbow and looking down at her.

'I'm thinking that I'm normally in bed at this hour.'

'You *are* in bed.'

'In bed and asleep,' she amended, laughing contentedly, the cat in full possession of the cream.

'And would you say that you're happy doing without your beauty sleep?' he asked lazily. She had satisfied him beyond expectation. After her initial apprehension, because the unknown was always so much scarier than the reality, she had been sexily and mind-blowingly responsive, thrilling at each touch, whimpering with the enjoyment of having him lavish her fulsome body with caresses. There was not an inch of her that he hadn't explored, and he had enjoyed every second of the exploration.

'I think it's made a very nice change,' she said demurely, and then laughed when he took offence and nipped her on the neck. He placed his hand squarely between her thighs and worked her flesh so that his knuckles grazed that already sensitised area.

She would have liked to be more expressive on the subject, but a part of her was still finding it hard to believe that this magnificent man was really interested in *her*. There was also a part of her that was nursing a small thought which had taken root at some point during their very long and very languid love-making session. It was a thought that filled her with a warm glow and for the moment she wanted to keep it to herself because, after all, this was the first night they had spent together. What if he got bored with her? He seemed to have a short attention span when it came to women, but Cristina wasn't going to dwell on that. Instead, she thought of how great it felt being in love, because she knew, with complete certainty, that she was in love with him.

Maybe he *had* had plenty of women in the past, maybe he had had an unhappy experience when he was young and foolishly married the wrong woman—but he was older now, and she liked to think that the very fact that she was so unlike the women who littered his past was promising.

'"Nice" is such a non-word,' Rafael chided. He replaced his hand with his thigh which he moved rhythmically between her legs.

'That's not your ego talking, is it?' she teased, half her attention focused on what was going on with her body, which was stirring into arousal even though they had barely stopped touching each other for the past few hours.

'We males are a fragile breed,' Rafael returned silkily.

'Perhaps I should say that it was earth shattering.'

'Now *that* is a definite improvement.' He cupped one heavy breast and then bent so that he could lick her nipple, which stiffened in immediate response. When he began suckling on it she gave a stifled groan and began moving against him, and this time they made love with hunger and urgency, their hands and mouths uniting as they explored each other's bodies. She did to him what he did to her, tasting him and enjoying his hardness, every inch of it.

She finally fell asleep and woke to a room flooded with sunlight and no sign of Rafael.

But there was a note. The note informed her that he would be in touch, and she carried it with her for the remainder of the day. Just having it on her made her heart sing. She literally felt light-headed with emotion and when, the following day, she picked up her telephone to hear his dark, velvety voice on the other end of the line, it was all she could do not to tell him just how very happy she was.

And events over the ensuing three months moved at the speed of light.

Rafael, she discovered, was not a man who did things in halves. He wanted her, and she was more than ready to accommodate him. Playing hard to get was not in her repertoire of feminine wiles, even when Anthea, who had viewed the proceedings with jaundiced eyes, told her that Rafael didn't appear to be the sort of man who would feel comfortable wearing an apron and putting out the garbage.

'He'll never have to wear an apron!' Cristina laughed. 'Why would he?'

'What a lucky man,' Anthea said wryly. 'Most women expect their guys to share the duties.'

'I really enjoy cooking,' Cristina told her, hurt by the implication that she was somehow lacking. True, she knew that she held very old-fashioned values, but that wasn't necessarily a bad thing, was it?

'And have you done much of that?'

'None,' Cristina confessed. 'I've offered, but—'

'But he's a man who prefers to dine out?' In the time they had been working together they had become firm friends, and, although their ages were close enough, Anthea was streets ahead when it came to men. Normally Cristina would have paid great attention to what her friend said, but when it came to Rafael she would allow no criticism. Anthea, she thought, was jaded from the bad experiences she had had with men. She also was not privy to the man behind that forbidding mask: the man who treated her with respect and consideration, the man who made love to her, always making sure that her needs were met ahead of his, the man who, yes, guarded his thoughts, but still managed to laugh at the things she said, the man who'd told her that she was wonderfully uncomplicated, the man who had encouraged her football coaching, even occasionally taking time out to come and see her.

'I'm just asking you to be careful.' Anthea relented, seeing the anxious expression on her friend's face. Cristina's open, trusting nature was at once both a blessing and a curse, as far as Anthea was concerned. Yes, her heart was fashioned out of pure gold, but it was a heart that could easily be broken, and Anthea had visited too many dodgy characters in the past not to know that someone like Rafael Rocchi would not be in it for the long haul. Not with a girl like Cristina who, rich in her own right though she might be, was not the ornamental bauble he would eventually like to dangle on his arm.

She had even been on the Internet and found pages upon pages on him, including a wide variety of pictures which had almost universally featured him with just those ornamental baubles she had expected to find. She had kept all of that to herself, but in her head a very clear picture had been formed of the sort of man he was.

'I mean,' she suggested kindly, 'Would it be the end of the world if you edged the conversation towards a future?'

Cristina, who had been mulling over that very question for the past couple of weeks, decided that yet again fate was at work, putting the thought firmly in the foreground.

She took more than usual care with her outfit that evening. Rafael had been away for the past three days, a flying visit to Boston. He was, he had told her over the telephone, really dying to see her. He was not averse to having long, sexy conversations with her on the phone, conversations that made her toes curls when she later recalled them. Cristina predicted that he would be in a very good mood when he came over.

They had planned on a meal out, as normal. After a flurry of trying different restaurants, they had now narrowed the field to a few of their favourites. Occasionally they skipped eating altogether, when the draw of the bedroom was simply too irresistible.

Today, however, Cristina had left work especially early to cook a meal. Fish, because she was still eternally watching her weight, and vegetables prepared exactly how she had been taught by their chef at home when she'd been growing up. Everything organic, of course, and everything bathed in a wonderful atmosphere thanks to some terrific smelly candles which she had found at a tiny little shop only round the corner.

As she took a last look at her reflection, liking the way the black dress cunningly hid what she still considered serious love-handles—never mind Rafael's flattery to the contrary—she felt her stomach flip over with a sudden attack of nerves.

She had been blissfully happy. Rafael fulfilled every part of her. He was her sounding board and her soul mate, but Anthea's blunt words of caution had managed to seep their way into her head, filling her with doubts. It seemed pretty early in the relationship for them to be discussing a future, but then again—and here she recalled yet more words of wisdom from one of the magazines she had devoured in the past— weren't two people in love supposed to know early on whether they wanted to commit to one another or not? She was sure she had read somewhere that relationships could drift for years, going apparently nowhere, only for one of the partners to break it off and within weeks to be married to someone else.

When Cristina tried to think of life without Rafael, her mind went blank and she felt cold with fear.

That fear, she reasoned now, could only be assuaged if she took the bull by the horns and did as Anthea had suggested.

For a few seconds, waiting for Rafael, she was filled with self-righteous courage, but as soon as she heard him phone up to her, her stomach went back to its antics, and she was busily wondering whether the meal had been such a good idea by the time he knocked on her door.

All her thoughts were scattered to the four winds the minute she set eyes on him.

He had come directly from the airport, was still carrying his overnight bag, along with the black case. Outside the weather was beautifully mild for the middle of May, and he had cuffed the sleeves of his shirt to his elbows. He looked lean and bronzed and muscular, and she felt that familiar leap of excitement as she looked at him.

Then he bent and kissed her, taking his time as he always did, his mouth making promises he would fulfil later in bed.

Only after he had straightened did he glance behind her into the tiny hall.

'What's the smell?'

'Smell?' Anthea's words of wisdom were fading fast as he stepped past her and glanced up the stairs in the direction of the kitchen. 'Oh, *that* smell!' She clapped her hand to her forehead in a casual gesture. 'I thought I'd cook. I know we'd booked to go out to that Italian, but all this eating out that we do…I'm not sure I'm getting the right balance of…um…nutrients anyway.' He was heading up the stairs and she hurriedly followed him, cursing herself for the linen, the crystal wine-glasses and the candles which were burning merrily away. Hardly the image of a meal whipped up by someone solely for nutritional purposes.

'Anyway!' she called up, shoving aside visions of him horrified by this show of domesticity, which he had not once suggested. 'I thought I'd just…' she caught her breath and watched him as he stood there in the small kitchen, surveying the carefully laid table, complete with the hateful candles '…whip up a meal for us. Nothing fancy.' She bit her lip nervously and hovered. 'I don't mind if you'd rather go out,' she finished lamely, but when he turned to her he was smiling, a slow smile as though something had clicked in his head.

'No way. Smells too good to pass up.' He walked towards her and gathered her in his arms. 'I didn't realise that cooking was another of your specialities.' Another tick in what had become a pleasingly traditional package. Cristina was a homemaker, and as far removed from the women he had dated in the past as chalk was from cheese.

Cristina breathed a sigh of relief. 'I wouldn't say a *speciality.*'

'Have I got time for a shower?' She had dressed for him. She had cooked for him. Normally those two things in combination would have had him running a mile, but with home and hearth on the agenda, they added up to just what he needed. A woman programmed to put her man first, a woman set in completely the opposite mould to that of his first wife. The fact that she turned him on was a distinct bonus, and he didn't dwell on what would happen when his boredom threshold was breached. That bridge would be crossed when he came to it. 'I don't suppose you fancy another?' His eyes swept appreciatively over her. He enjoyed showering with her, enjoyed their slippery bodies rubbing together under the fine, warm spray.

'I'll start with the meal.' She remembered what Anthea had said about modern women expecting duties to be shared equally with their men. 'You can come and help when you're ready. If you want. I've pretty much done it all, as a matter of fact.' She wondered where she was going with this. And now he was looking at her with that indulgent expression he sometimes wore, which she'd interpreted as the grown-up tolerating the antics of a kid.

She was ready with the starters by the time he emerged twenty minutes later from the shower, his hair still damp and swept back, and wearing a pair of jeans and a black tee shirt. He had never brought clothes to her house, but over time she had accumulated some, left and laundered and carefully put in one of the cupboards in the spare room. She had taken it, subconsciously, as a hopeful sign that he hadn't removed them, but had dipped into them, taking it for granted that he would have one or two essentials on tap.

Rafael felt wonderfully relaxed. He made a token effort to do something with a bowl of lettuce leaves and some spring onions, but in the end contented himself with pouring them both a glass of wine and sitting down at the kitchen table so that he could watch her as she bustled around the kitchen, checking things and fetching crockery down from the cupboards.

He found her tide of chirpy chatter as entertaining as it was soothing. For someone who worked in a flower shop and did football coaching once a week, she always seemed bursting with news—things she had seen during her day, the random people she had chatted to, thoughts and plans that had flitted through her head and which she'd told him she liked to discuss with him. He was amazed that it didn't irritate the hell out of him, but it didn't. She was easily pleased and he found that he liked that. In the general scheme of things, the less easily pleased the woman, the shorter the relationship.

Now she was chatting to him about the starter, which was a combination of various seafoods in a spicy tomato sauce and served in a large glass bowl stuffed with crisp lettuce and tomatoes.

'Am I boring you?' she asked out of the blue, and Rafael looked at her quizzically.

'Why would you ask that?'

'Because I seem to be the one doing all the talking, and…' She tucked her hair behind her ear and looked at him earnestly. 'I just wondered whether you find it a bit dull listening to me rattle on about the silly things that happen in my life, when you'd probably much rather be talking about more important stuff.'

Rafael speared a prawn on his fork and held it out to her to nibble. She had a very sexy mouth and a very sexy way of eating food. She didn't view it as a plateful of calories waiting to pounce. She enjoyed every mouthful of what she ate, and it was a turn-on just watching her.

This time, however, she shook her head and stared down at her plate for a few seconds.

'I enjoy not talking about "important stuff",' Rafael told her. 'I spend countless hours talking about *important stuff*. It's great to get here and listen to you tell me about the latest drama in your life.'

'I don't have a dramatic life, Rafael. You do.'

'On the contrary.' He finished his starter and stood up to clear the table. 'I listen to stockbrokers and bankers and lawyers discuss technicalities of management buyouts and takeover bids and foreign currency markets. Hardly drama.'

That sounded pretty dramatic to Cristina, whose mind seemed to shut down the second it was presented with a financial problem. Anthea had turned out to be a godsend in that area, handling all the accounts efficiently and expertly. Normally she would have chattered away to him about her lack of ability when it came to sorting out money matters. He'd often teased her about that. But now, on her pressing bandwagon of trying to find out where they were going, and with Anthea's warning words ringing in her ears, she lapsed into anxious silence.

'What did you talk to…your other girlfriends about?' she asked eventually, and he frowned at her.

'How am I supposed to remember?' She seemed to be lost in a little worried world of her own, so he fetched the fish from the oven and gestured for her to remain seated while he dished out. 'Now.' He sat down and looked at her steadily. 'What's this all about?'

Now or never. She took a deep breath and reminded herself that she had never been the sort of girl who was willing to be dangled on a string, waiting for a day that might never arrive. She had old-fashioned principles, and already she was in the process of jettisoning them by sleeping with Rafael when she had no real idea where they were heading. She had fallen instantly and madly in love with him and, while that love was glorious and uplifting, it had also cleverly ambushed a lifetime's worth of romantic convictions and beliefs.

'Rafael…I really need to know where we're going. I mean,' she continued hurriedly, 'I never planned to get involved in a relationship that was going nowhere.' Underneath the kitchen table, she wrung her hands together and mentally told herself that she was absolutely doing the right thing. 'I've told Mum and Dad about us, and they haven't said anything, but I know that they don't approve. This may sound silly to you, but...' Those amazing blue eyes were narrowed on her and she didn't have a clue what was going on in his head. She had seen that look a few times when he had taken work calls in her presence, that inscrutable, shuttered look that lent him an air of chilling foreboding. Directed at her, she felt her stomach spasm into painful knots as she desperately tried to hang on to her courage.

'But...?'

'But I haven't been brought up to sleep my way through a series of meaningless relationships.' Another lungful of air. 'I...' She almost slipped up and told him that she loved him, but she bit back the words which, even more than the carefully planned meal, would have guaranteed him running scared within seconds. He had not once mentioned love, and she wasn't going to ask for declarations, just for the hope that they could progress the relationship in the right direction.

'And that's a good thing,' he surprised her by

saying. He leaned across the table towards her. The first time he had proposed marriage, he had done it in style—bended knee, his mother's engagement ring. That marriage had been an illusion. This, however, was reality and there would be no foolish romantic gestures. 'I don't expect you to continue sleeping with me, assuming the position of mistress. I knew that the very first time we slept together it was a matter of great significance for you.' He paused. 'I would never disrespect you, nor would I disrespect your parents by stringing you along. Which is why I think we should get married.'

'*Get married?*'

'Of course.'

This wasn't what Cristina had imagined, not as a marriage proposal nor, for that matter, as a likely outcome for her conversation with him. Gradually, though, his words sunk in. Not only was he prepared to offer her hope that their relationship was more serious than she could ever have dreamed possible, but he was proving it by doing the one thing he had spent years avoiding! It might have been a bit flat as far as proposals went, but he wasn't given to sweeping emotional displays, and wasn't this her dream come true? Her fairy-tale ending?

She smiled tentatively and he took her hand and idly played with her wedding finger. 'So…is that a yes?' he asked softly.

'It's a yes!'

'Good.' Rafael sat back, satisfied. 'In that case, a ring is in order. I think it's safe to say that we might as well enjoy a brief spell of calm before our families are let loose.'

That funny, flat feeling was gone as her imagination took wing and began to soar. *A ring!* She would be sporting an engagement ring! And would be marrying the man of her dreams! *How much better could life get?*

She went across and flung her arms around him. 'Does that mean,' he drawled, 'That you're offering yourself for dessert?'

'Just making the most of this brief spell of calm, as you ordered,' Cristina laughed. 'And, in case you're still hungry, you can have whatever dessert you like…'

CHAPTER SIX

IN ALL good movies, the dashing man proposed on bended knee, flourishing an antique engagement ring, which magically always fitted the blushing bride-to-be. Sometimes the ring was concealed in a fortune cookie, which had always got Cristina wondering what might happen if it were to be accidentally swallowed.

She decided that it was probably much better to actually choose the engagement ring together and, Rafael being Rafael, the minute she had accepted his marriage proposal he took charge.

He knew exactly which jewellers to visit, as he had used them himself in the past. Cristina wondered what, exactly, he had bought from them, but she kept that uneasy question to herself, happy to go along with the flow. Despite owning some valuable pieces of jewellery herself, most of which were pointlessly locked in bank vaults, Cristina was not a jewellery person. Rings and necklaces might look fine on her sisters, but she personally found that they got in the way of normal day-to-day activities, like gardening or playing sports. How on earth could she coach football with a tiara on her head or a string of pearls wrapped around her neck?

'We'll try and stay away from the flamboyant pieces, in that case,' Rafael had told her. But when, two days later, they found themselves in the exclusive jewellery shop, Cristina watched in dismay as drawers of rings with diamonds the size of oranges were pulled out.

'You know, I could always get it from one of Dad's shops in Italy,' she said faintly, staring down at something that glittered so much she felt she might need to fetch her sunglasses out of her handbag.

'Nonsense. What's wrong with the selection here?'

'Remember what I said about not really liking rings with diamonds the size of rocks?' She picked out one of the smaller pieces and held it up. It was a good diamond, but it was still a very large diamond. The man clucking around them had discreetly positioned himself to one side and Cristina turned to Rafael awkwardly.

'We could always go for something really cheap and cheerful,' she joked. 'That way, when I get knocked football coaching, it won't matter too much if it falls off.'

Rafael frowned. 'What do you mean, when you get knocked football coaching?'

'It happens.' Cristina broke it to him in a teasing voice. 'Running around on a muddy playing field with a bunch of teenagers trying to score a goal. Sometimes they don't see me on the sidelines shouting instructions. Or maybe they do.' She laughed, expecting him to laugh back with her, but instead his ebony brows were knitted into a frown. 'What's the matter?' she asked, slotting the ring back into its velvet niche and signalling for the proprietor to take the case away.

'Why would you be football coaching?' Rafael asked with genuine puzzlement in his voice.

'Ah.' Cristina was beginning to understand. She turned to the proprietor with a smile. 'We're going to go away for a bit and think about which ring is right for us,' she said. 'Rafael, shall we go and grab something to eat and we can discuss this?'

'What's there to discuss? There must be a ring in this shop that you like, Cristina.'

'Come on.' She placed her small hand on his arm and guided him out of the shop into the bright sunlight outside. A sunny Saturday in London was not the most relaxing place on the face of the earth to be. The streets were overflowing with people, tourists snapping pictures, young girls frantically trying to shop, people scurrying to destinations unknown, and all of them in a terrible rush from the looks of it.

Across the street was a coffee shop, one of those new-fangled ones that sold fancy coffees with long names and over sized prices, along with paninis, baguettes and tiny salads in eco-friendly packaging.

'Look, Rafael,' she opened, when they had finally emerged from the queue and were sitting in front of their tall paper cups of coffee. 'There's something we need to talk about.' She took a careful sip of her latte and thought about what she was going to say. This was something she had never considered when she had joyfully accepted his proposal of marriage. Rafael was all Italian, and his way of looking at marriage had been through the eyes of a man who could see no reason for his wife to work. Not only could he more than afford to keep her in whatever style she so desired, but that would be his right and his duty. It would make no difference that she could more than afford to keep herself in whatever style she chose. He was Italian, and that would be the way things would work.

She took a deep breath. 'I love what I do, Rafael. I came over here so that I could open my flower shop and try and fulfil some of my ambitions. I know that, next to yours, you probably find my ambitions a little limp, but there's no way I am going to give up everything I've worked for the minute there's a ring on my finger.'

Rafael frowned. 'I see no reason for my wife to go out to work,' he said heavily.

'That's a very Victorian point of view. This is the twenty-first century. Women go out to work. They don't stay indoors doing the cooking and cleaning and laundry and waiting for their husbands to come through the front door at the end of the day.' She thought that Anthea would have been very proud of that little speech. Of course, compared to her friend, she was alarmingly old-fashioned, but Rafael… Rafael was a positive dinosaur.

'I'm not asking you to do the cooking and cleaning and laundry,' he now pointed out. 'I have my own chef, and someone comes in twice a week to do the cleaning and laundry. Actually, it won't be a problem if she comes in every day. I'm sure she would be more than amenable if she's offered enough money.'

'And what would I do all day?' Cristina asked, knowing that she should be angry with him for his out-dated attitude, but warmly aware that there was a note of possessiveness behind it that thrilled her to death.

Rafael shrugged. 'Whatever women who don't go out to work do all day.' He wouldn't go into too many details on that one. His dearest ex-wife had managed to pack in a surprising amount in her days. Unlike Cristina, she had been more than happy to ditch her job and begin the arduous marital task of running through vast sums of money. Along the way—and seemingly immune to the stunningly obvious piece of logic which states that a man must work in order to earn— she had grown bored with a husband who was always at work, bored with random spending, and had taken to distributing her favours else-where, on men who'd flattered her ego and filled the increasing absences of her husband.

Ironically Cristina, who came with money of her own and didn't have a need to work, was the one now insinuating that he was something from the Dark Ages because he wanted a wife at home.

'I wouldn't know,' Cristina told him. 'I've never just stayed at home and done nothing.'

'What do your sisters do?'

'Rafael, they both have children and very busy lives. Frankie does a lot of charity stuff, organ-ising events, and they both play tennis and golf.'

Rafael tried and failed to picture Cristina playing tennis, followed by tea with a select group of friends. She wasn't a tennis-playing kind of person.

'I'm going to keep running the flower shop,' she stated firmly. 'And I'm also going to carry on with the football coaching when the season begins towards the end of the year. And I might just have my first commission to landscape a garden in July. So, before we get married and I disappoint you, I might as well say that I won't be giving up my various jobs.'

'I don't feel comfortable having a wife who's running all over London working for other people.'

Cristina, knowing exactly the way his mind was working, released a small sigh. 'I won't be running all over London working for other people,' she told him mildly.

'Landscape jobs?'

'One possible landscape job.'

'You'll be all over the country. Sourcing baby conifers and spring bulbs.'

Cristina laughed out loud. 'You don't know the first thing about gardening, do you?

'Why on earth would I?'

'Well, I can assure you, a lot of it will be in the layout and design, and I really won't need to trek the length and breadth of the country to get whatever plants I may need.'

Rafael, having pretty much banked on an obedient and traditional wife, looked in some consternation at the stubborn set of her mouth. She might be sweetly undemanding, but it was obvious that she was capable of digging those sweetly undemanding heels in. He mentally conceded defeat in this particular area which, he had to admit, was not a particularly important area.

If she wanted to play at the flower-shop business, then so be it. The football coaching, or any other coaching for that matter, could simply be seen as a form of exercise, similar to going to the gym once a week. And, well, a landscape job… one that might or might not materialise…what was the use in getting stressed over that?

Also—and he came to the conclusion that this was of greater importance—what had his ex done in the absence of any job or hobby or overriding interest? The devil worked on idle hands.

All things considered, it might be a better thing for Cristina to potter around her flower shop and sketch layouts for other people's gardens.

He smiled magnanimously at her. 'You're right,' he said grandly. 'I've been brought up with the outmoded concept of the wife at home tending the fires.'

'While the caveman does the hunting,' she agreed, relieved that this minor difficulty had been surmounted. 'And I won't be needing a chef to do the cooking,' she continued. 'Although a cleaner might be useful now and again.'

'No, the chef is definitely redundant after that meal you cooked for me a couple of days ago.' He grinned at her. Cristina wondered whether he knew just how sexy he looked when he smiled like that, when the harsh angles of his face were softened and his eyes looked hot and lazy. 'I particularly enjoyed the dessert,' he added wickedly. 'What would you call it?'

'Ssh!' Cristina looked around her, blushing. *He* might think that because he viewed the rest of the world with royal indifference that it, likewise, was royally indifferent to *him*. Not so. Even in a heaving London coffee shop, he still managed to be the centre of attention, and Cristina was sure that a number of the women had deliberately decided to enjoy their coffees inside instead of taking them out. Rafael Rocchi made very fetching scenery.

'I can't believe you can be shy when you think—'

'That it's time to go!' She stood up, bright red, aware that a couple of women too close for comfort were listening with interest to their exchange.

'Of course. The ring. And then—' he stuck his hands in his pockets and stepped back, allowing her to precede him through the door '—I think a visit to the country might be in order. My mother will be over the moon.'

* * *

Cristina was blissfully happy on the drive up to the Lake District. It was hard to imagine that months ago she had undertaken exactly the same drive in her little Mini. Who ever would have thought that, with summer breaking through the cool spring days, she would now be making the same trip in Rafael's Bentley with a glorious, exciting future stretching out in front of her with the man she adored?

Three weeks ago they had finally chosen the engagement ring and she looked surreptitiously now at her finger where it sparkled, a tangible reminder that this wasn't all some weird dream from which she would eventually awaken.

He had refused to indulge her whimsy for something cheap and cheerful. Having been surrounded by jewellery all her life, she would have liked to discard the formality of something really expensive, but that, he had informed her, was inappropriate.

'My wife will wear the best,' he had said to her, squashing all thoughts of rebellion.

The diamond wasn't the size of a boulder, but it would never pass unnoticed. Utterly impractical for her line of work, but what was a loving relationship if not about compromises? And hadn't he compromised when it had come to her work?

Her parents had been overjoyed at the news of her engagement. In fact, like a rider pulling back on the reins of a runaway horse, Cristina had had to halt the tide of plans, which had included an elaborate engagement party in Italy, similar to the extravaganza which both her sisters had enjoyed. That had been *their* choice, but it wasn't hers. She remembered both parties as confusingly big affairs at which she had clung to the sidelines, sipping non-alcoholic drinks and wondering when she could slip away to her bedroom so that she could catch up on the reality TV show she had been obliged to miss.

It was already seven in the evening by the time they finally made it to Maria's country house. Cristina had spent much of the trip dozing, much to Rafael's amusement. He had never been known to send a woman to sleep, and he found that he rather missed her chatter, having become accustomed to her random remarks about perfectly ordinary things and perfectly dull-looking people. Sometimes in the past few weeks, when his day had been particularly gruelling, he had picked up the phone knowing that her good-natured, irrepressible small talk would soothe and entertain him.

'We're here,' he said, turning to her as he pulled into the drive and killed his engine. In a minute his mother would be outside, and he very much looked forward to a weekend spent without that insidious message being passed to him in silent but pointed waves that it was time for him to find himself a good wife and settle down. He had taken her advice and, hats off to his mother, he felt perfectly contented with his decision.

'Was I asleep?' Cristina asked, yawning.

'Asleep and snoring.'

'I wasn't!' She shot up into a sitting position and looked at him in horror, but grinned when she saw the expression on his face.

Rafael kissed her swiftly on the mouth. 'That's about all we'll be getting,' he murmured. 'At least while my mother has her beady eyes on us. She's never been one to approve of public displays of affection. I might just have to creep into your bedroom tonight under cover of darkness.' He glanced towards the front door and, as it was still shut, he slipped his hand under her shirt. No bra.

He touched one pert nipple with his thumb and felt her quicken and melt under the caress. Did he have time for more? He would have liked to shove that shirt up and fasten his mouth to that sweetly ripened, throbbing bud, would have liked to have her sink further down the plush leather seat so that he could ravish her in the cool, expensive elegance of his car.

Unfortunately…

He withdrew his hand with marked reluctance and took a few deep, steadying breaths because his body was already slamming into response. 'We'd better go inside,' he growled. 'Or else I'll be sorely tempted to reverse back down the drive and head for the nearest lay-by. Which wouldn't exactly be cool, now, would it?'

'Especially not when your mother's waving at us from the downstairs bay window.'

She smiled as Rafael jerked back and pushed open his car door, leaving her to try and calm her body's tempestuous reaction to his fondling. Making out in a car was strictly for teenagers, she had always thought. Definitely not cool when it came to adults. But if Maria hadn't appeared just then, and if he had driven his Bentley to the nearest lay-by, then she would have happily let him have his way with her.

Her skin prickled at the thought of them in his car, his head buried between her thighs, nuzzling at her breasts, claiming her mouth...

She'd never thought that she would see the day when she would need a cold shower, but that seemed to be the effect he had on her. One glance, a fleeting touch, and she melted like a candle over an open flame.

As Rafael had predicted—and she would have been surprised otherwise—they had been put in separate bedrooms, with the very long distance of hall and corridor between them. Maria belonged to that generation of adults, just as her parents did, who would never have contemplated their offspring sharing a bedroom with their current partner, even if the partner in question was sporting a very expensive engagement ring on her finger. No; the only ring that would have led to a king-sized bed prepared for two was of the wedding variety.

But on Cloud Nine, which was currently

Cristina's address, it was of little importance. She had the rest of her life to enjoy getting to know the man she was going to marry. A couple of nights under the same roof but in separate beds was not going to be unduly stressful.

She was also looking forward to getting to know Maria a little better as well. And she was pleased that they were going to be staying in, enjoying a home-cooked meal, instead of going to a restaurant.

'Of course,' she confided as she guiltily tucked into a second helping of Maria's exceptional home-made lasagne, 'I really shouldn't be indulging in this.' She sighed. 'Too much cheese. Very bad for the figure.' There was also tiramisu for dessert. Cristina had spied it sitting temptingly in the fridge earlier on and, ruthlessly honest as she was with her own eating habits, she'd known that she would be indulging. Then there had been the wine. Very dry and very cold and very drinkable. She had had three glasses and was feeling pleasantly relaxed. The conversation had flowed, with Rafael at his most witty and charming, Maria had chatted about incidents in her youthful past that had featured her friends and Cristina's parents, and it was all so very comfortable that she'd had to pinch herself a couple of times just to make sure that this was really happening.

'Nonsense,' Maria laughed. 'You have a real figure.' She wagged one finger warningly. 'Men don't like this stick-insect woman,' she said, smiling. 'A real man likes a woman with some substance!'

Rafael was laughing as he left the dining room carrying an armful of plates and Maria turned to Cristina and said fondly, 'I cannot tell you how pleased I am that that son of mine finally listened to what I told him.'

'What's that?'

Maria covered Cristina's hand with her own and gave it a little squeeze of affection.

'About settling down. I told him that he would become a sad, lonely old man if he didn't find himself a suitable wife, and for once he listened to what I had to say! And, I must say,' she added with a hint of complacency in her voice, 'I couldn't have picked a better daughter-in-law myself! Now, my dear—' she stood up and yawned '—I am going to leave you two young things…dessert in the fridge… old lady like me…'

Cristina heard Maria's voice as just a background whisper barely audible above the roaring in her ears. Yes, yes, yes… She was nodding as if her mind wasn't exploding, agreeing with Maria that indeed she would have some of the tiramisu, that she knew where her bedroom was, that she shouldn't be too late up because there were plans to go to the market the following day…sunshine predicted…another warm one…

Five minutes ago she had heard Rafael doing domestic things in the kitchen and she had felt utterly and completely happy. Now she wanted to lock the dining room door, shut him out until she could assimilate what Maria had said—those casual, throwaway words about finding a *suitable wife*.

Cristina remembered that surreal feeling she had had, that a man like Rafael, so supremely *eligible*, could ever have managed to be attracted to *her*. He had made her feel sexy and desirable, but really and truly, when she looked in the mirror, she didn't see the sort of woman she would have associated with him. And now, in the stillness of the dining room, all of Anthea's warnings came flooding back to her, washing away her happiness like footprints on a beach.

She felt the sting of tears prick behind her eyes, and she wanted to duck down under the table and hide until she could sneak away from the house, back to the safety of her own apartment, where she might be able to get her chaotic thoughts back into some sort of order.

Rafael had never once told her that he loved her, but like a fool, she hadn't let that stand in the way of believing that he did, that he *must*, because why else would he have asked her to marry him?

She cast her fevered mind back to his proposal. She had laughed at herself at the time for expecting something romantic, and had simply accepted that he wasn't the romantic type—not the sort to kneel and slip the antique ring on her finger, not the sort to wax lyrical about having her for his wife.

She heard the sound of his approaching footsteps and looked up from where she was sitting in frozen silence. He had a tea cloth slung over one shoulder, the picture of the domestic man. But looks, as she now knew, could be deceiving. Rafael was no more domestic than a jungle animal, although he was willing to dabble if he had to.

Rafael paused at the door to the dining room, his antennae picking up something, although he wasn't sure what. He frowned and slowly began clearing the rest of the dishes from the table, expecting her to stand up and give him a hand. She normally did this sort of stuff. She didn't. Instead she remained where she was, staring down at the remnants of the food, as if looking for the table to provide answers to some internal question.

'What's the matter?' Rafael asked, relegating any disquiet to the back of his mind. He swung round to stand behind her and then he leaned forward and kissed the side of her neck. His mother was safely tucked up in her bed, and the thought of having the place to themselves made him feel horny. Being at his mother's house, knowing that he had done the one thing in the world guaranteed to make her happy, was as rewarding as he had anticipated. His mother heartily approved of Cristina, and he had been spared those prickly conversations about his future which he had always found frustrating.

'All is quiet on the western front,' he murmured seductively into her ear, but where she once would have squirmed with pleasure Cristina now pulled away slightly and twisted around to face him.

'I…I don't feel comfortable, not when we're here in your mother's house…'

'*Now* who's being the dinosaur?' Rafael teased her. 'My mother has retired early for a reason. She may not openly condone us sleeping together, but she isn't a fool.' But that little ripple of disquiet showed its teeth once again.

It took all of her will power not to succumb to his massive charm. Or for that matter to her treacherous body, which was doing its own thing, ignoring what her head was telling it to do. She stood up and did a funny little side step out of his embrace, then she began clearing the rest of the plates, eyes averted.

Rafael followed her into the kitchen where he had made a rudimentary attempt to load the dishwasher, but unsurprisingly, had only managed to stick in the plates and cutlery, leaving all things difficult piled up in the sink.

'I'll finish these off,' Cristina said quietly, looking at the pile of dirty dishes instead of at him. 'You can head up to bed. You must be exhausted after all that driving.'

'I like it when you look at me when you talk,' Rafael drawled. 'Or are you in one of those mysterious moods which women seem prone to?'

Cristina felt an unaccustomed surge of rage rush through her, and she gritted her teeth together to suppress the awful desire to shout at him.

'You should know about women and their mysterious moods,' she muttered violently instead, and she felt Rafael still behind her.

'Meaning…?' He rested his hands on her shoulders and swivelled her around so that she was forced to at least face his direction, although she cravenly kept her eyes pinned to the flag-tiled kitchen floor.

Cristina took a deep breath and dived straight in. What choice did she have? She could continue making mysterious and bitter asides, but the truth was that sooner or later she would have to confront the issue and, who knew? Maybe she had misinterpreted Maria, or misheard. She had a fleeting moment's peace of mind at the thought of that, of a perfectly harmless, innocent remark having been taken *out of context* and cruelly magnified into something *suspicious*.

'Your mother and I were having a little chat while you were in the kitchen.'

'Oh, yes?'

'It's just that she said… Well, she mentioned something in passing that I need to talk to you about.'

'I can think of better things to do than talk.'

'I know I'm probably being over-imaginative…'

Rafael resigned himself to one of those conversations in which, he knew, only ten percent of his mind would actively participate. It would probably involve wedding preparations or something equally tedious and, whilst he would dearly have liked to distract her, he could tell from the stubborn angle of her head that this was important to her and he shrugged, dropping the tea cloth on the counter.

'Okay. Do you want some of that dessert in the fridge?'

Cristina thought of Maria's description of her, fondly intentioned but unwittingly cutting. *A real woman*. Cristina didn't particularly want to be *a real woman*. Right now, she would happily have settled for Barbie-doll status, because, despite what Maria had said, men weren't attracted to *real women*. How could she have been so blind as to imagine that Rafael was seriously attracted to her? She was a novelty at the moment, and he was probably making the best of a bad job in sleeping with the woman he had more or less been set up to marry. Just thinking about it now made her head swim and her legs feel weak.

'I'm fine.'

'Now I really *am* concerned.'

'This is serious, Rafael,' Cristina said more sharply than she was accustomed to, and he frowned at her. She could see him trying to work out what was going on and she realised, belatedly, how transparently predictable she had been—always thrilled to see him, always ready to make love, always sunny natured because that was her temperament. He had beckoned, and like someone in a trance she had walked towards him, never asking all those questions which she now realised she should have been asking.

Frankly, she had been clueless.

'Could we go into the sitting room?' she asked.

'As you wish.'

Cristina nodded and led the way. It was a grand house, but many of the rooms downstairs were shut up because Maria, on her own, really only occupied the kitchen, the cosy den which she used as her office, the sitting room and her bedroom. In summer, she said that she liked nothing better than her garden room at the back, from which she could contemplate the beauty of nature. Consequently, those rooms which were used all year round were cluttered and cosy and quite different from the remainder of the house.

With the foundations of her fairy-tale future disappearing like a puff of smoke in a high wind, Cristina was piecing together all those missing jigsaw pieces which she had cheerfully ignored. For instance, she thought bitterly, how odd had it been that after only three months he had proposed marriage—a man accustomed to single life in the fast lane, surrounded by the most beautiful women in the world, sought after, courted, desired? How was it that he had suddenly decided to wave goodbye to all of that in a matter of *a few seconds,* so to speak, because *she*, plump, gauche and nothing stunning in the looks department, had come along?

'You were saying?'

Cristina, lost in her thoughts, had almost forgotten what she had been saying. She focused her eyes on the man sitting next to her on the sofa and blinked.

'I was saying that your mother… Maria said something and I need you to clarify.'

'Get to the point, Cristina.'

Was he being understandably impatient because she was waffling, *or were these just the signs of arrogance which she had conveniently chosen to overlook but which had been there all along?*

'She said that she was really happy…that you had decided to finally settle down…'

'And so she is. Are we going somewhere with this or is it just the circles thing?'

'She said that she had spoken to you…told you that it was time that you found *a suitable wife.*' Bitterness had crept into her voice, and Rafael's face darkened. 'I need to find out what this is all about, Rafael,' she pursued doggedly. 'Finding a suitable wife. Is that what this is all about?' The words were wrenched out of her and spoken straight from the heart.

'You're beginning to sound hysterical, Cristina, and I don't do hysterics.'

'I'm not being hysterical. I'm just asking you to tell me the truth, whether you were put up to this.'

'I don't think I like that expression,' Rafael said, his lean, handsome face taut.

'Well, I can't think of another one to use. Your mother said that she told you that it was time to find *a suitable wife* and, lo and behold, here I am!'

'You seem to have a problem with that term and I don't understand why.' The relaxing weekend Rafael had anticipated seemed to be going rapidly pear-shaped and he was at a loss to explain why. Cristina, so obliging for the past few months, was now asking questions which he personally found unnecessary, and standing her ground. Why? She should have been *pleased* that he considered her a suitable wife! He had already been through a wife who had been totally unsuitable. What higher compliment than to be chosen for her suitability?

Cristina's hope that she had somehow misinterpreted Maria's remark crumbled into ashes.

'Yes, my mother suggested that it was time I settled down and I agreed with her.' He gave a casual, elegant shrug. 'Where is the problem in that? There comes a moment in every man's life when he must weigh the advantages of playing hard against the peace of tying the knot.'

Cristina had a mental image of a pair of scales with 'Fun and Frolics' on one side and herself, 'Giant Knot', on the other. No love to be seen and, without love, how long before 'Giant Knot' lost its appeal? Would he then expect to resume his fun and frolics, with the added bonus of having Giant Knot at home raising children, cooking meals and waiting for him to return?

'So this would be a bit like a business transaction, in other words?'

'Why do you insist on using such emotive language?' Rafael enquired impatiently.

Cristina turned away, the sting of tears making her blink rapidly, willing herself not to cry because she was pretty sure that he probably didn't do crying along with hysterics.

'It's not going to work.' She wriggled the engagement ring from her finger, turned back to him and silently held out her hand with the ring in her palm. 'The diamond was too big anyway. How could I do football coaching or my flowers wearing it?' She forced herself to smile in the face of his stony expression. 'I should have seen that as a sign. We couldn't even agree on the ring.'

CHAPTER SEVEN

THE evening and following day were a nightmare of misery and tension. Cristina had handed Rafael back his ring, but he had refused to accept it. Instead, he had looked at her with a long, cool expression and told her to consider the implications of not wearing it. The explanations to his mother, which would be uncomfortable at the very best. What would she say—that they had had a massive row and she had decided to call the whole thing off? His mother, he had assured her, would smile indulgently and probably tell her something wise about pre-wedding nerves. Or else she could go for the truth, tell his mother…that what? She considered herself at the wrong end of a deal which she had now decided she didn't care for—a deal to marry one of the most eligible men in the world?

'Wear the ring,' he had told her. 'We can discuss this later.'

Coward that she was, Cristina, faced with the scenario which Rafael had succinctly depicted in sparse but extremely graphic detail, had silently slipped the ring back onto her finger, but it had felt like barbed wire against her skin.

She had smiled, and the following day had limped by, each minute feeling like a lifetime, until finally, at four in the evening, they'd been standing by the door with their cases by their feet, ready to face the long journey back to London.

She had managed to successfully avoid 'the cosy chat' situation by disappearing outside at all available opportunities, and then reappearing with the excuse that she was seeking inspiration for her landscape project, that she couldn't get enough of the countryside. Towards the end Maria had been eyeing her with a puzzled expression, and Cristina had realised that she'd been walking the thin line between appearing engagingly committed to her ambitions and a complete lunatic.

She gave Maria a hug of genuine warmth, and suddenly a small but promising idea presented itself to her. Here she was, idiotically in love with a man who felt nothing for her but a temporary attraction, a man who saw her as a suitable partner. On paper, she made sense— right background, right connections, even the added bonus of a history among parents. He would marry her because, like any sensible investment, she would stand the test of time. He hadn't banked on her response on discovering that she was a useful commodity. In fact, he hadn't banked on her *finding out* that little gem, although it wouldn't have worried him unduly if she had, because it would never have occurred to him that she wouldn't go along for the ride. Well connected she might be, but she was no model, nor did she have the finesse of someone whose life had been relatively pampered. He had probably imagined that her gratitude would take her right up to the altar and beyond, whatever his reasons for marrying her.

This was an engagement from which she had to wriggle out with as much subtlety as she could muster, because to admit to anyone that she was marrying a man who saw her as a sensible *investment*… Well, she would sooner have grabbed the nearest spade, dug a hole for herself and jumped in. The humiliation would have been unendurable. Her sisters would have smiled sympathetically and encouraged her to go along with it because, after all, she wasn't getting any younger. But behind her back they would have shaken their heads in sympathy and thanked their lucky stars that they'd been blessed with husbands who had genuinely been attracted to them.

And her parents would have supported her, of course, but they too would have retired to their bedroom and, with no one around to hear them, lamented the fact that their poor baby would never know the meaning of true love.

Frankly, it was too horrible to think about, and her only solution was to extricate herself with as much dignity as she could.

She beamed at Maria and stood back, her hands resting lightly on Maria's arms. Out of the corner of her eye, she could see that hateful diamond glittering mockingly at her, and she sighed.

'I can't tell you how wonderful it's been coming up here.' She allowed her eyes to linger on the magnificent landscape. The extensive acreage, lawned and forested, blended seamlessly into the fields and open countryside, giving you the feeling that you were, indeed, mistress of all you surveyed.

'London has a buzz,' she said, allowing a note of wistful sadness to creep into her voice—and at the back of her mind wondering whence she had dredged her acting skills, she who had always felt so strongly that playing games was a waste of time. 'But my heart really belongs in the country.'

'I can tell,' Maria said wryly.

'Oh, you mean you've noticed? I wasn't *that* obvious, was I?' She glanced at Rafael standing alongside her and looked away hurriedly at his raised brows. 'Rafael and I have discussed this so many times…the fact that I can't bear the thought of living in London for the rest of my days…'

'You're only young, my dear.'

'I know!' Cristina interjected, determined to capitalise on whatever headway she had gained. 'But I like to think ahead. The bigger picture and all that.' She fiddled with the lump of rock on her finger. 'I really had only planned on living in London for a brief time, until I found my feet over here. It seemed the most promising place to start, and I was right; my flower shop is doing great. In fact, Anthea and I, well, we've actually thought about extending it, opening another shop—maybe incorporating a landscape-design service. And naturally we would want to do that somewhere in the country. Anthea's from the country herself… Well, the New Forest area, in actual fact—not entirely sure where that is…quite rural, I gather…' She could feel herself losing sight of her original purpose, which had been to build for herself the foundations for her eventual escape from the predicament in which she now found herself.

'You have ambitions…that's good. So many young women these days are content to squander the money their parents have worked hard to earn, and then they wonder why they aren't happy.' Maria looked at Rafael, and Cristina knew that she was thinking about her son's ex-wife and the lavish lifestyle which had brought her no happiness. This was not the right road. She didn't want to be considered some kind of paragon of virtue and, before any favourable comparisons could be made, she broke in firmly.

'The dilemma of where I would want to live, well, that's a big one…best left for another time, I guess. I'm just hoping that it's one that can be sorted…but enough of all that.' She made a show of looking at her watch and then suggested that perhaps it was time to leave.

'That,' Rafael said as the house disappeared from view, 'Was a moderately convincing performance.'

'Here is the ring back. I can't bear having it on my finger.' She wriggled it off and dropped it neatly on the shiny walnut gear-box. The thing had cost an arm and a leg, but instead of taking it Rafael barely gave it a glance. She thought that he had, perhaps, made a crucial mistake in choosing her. He had assumed that her privileged background would work in his favour. Just one more tick in the box. However, had she been from a less advantaged background, then his casual dismissal of that fantastically expensive ring now juddering as the car picked up speed would have impressed her to death. She hoped not sufficiently for her to have ignored her broken heart, but who knew?

With no one around, she felt that surge of hurt and anger rush through her once more.

'You're making a mistake,' Rafael said conversationally, his eyes focused on the strip of road ahead.

Cristina had determined to maintain a dignified

silence for the duration of the journey—after all she had already said what she'd needed to—but there was no way that she was going to let that remark go unanswered. She turned to him and valiantly squashed that little flip her stomach did whenever her eyes were confronted with the sheer beauty of his face. The last thing she needed was to be ambushed by her body.

'I would have been making the biggest mistake of my life if I had married you,' she said bitterly.

'How do you figure that?'

'I…' She drew in a trembling breath and blinked rapidly to clear the watery film from her eyes. 'I thought we had something special—'

'There are tissues in the glove compartment.'

'How can you be so…so…*cold*!' Cristina yelled, shocked by this newly found capacity for rage. Where had that placid person gone— The one who was always upbeat and never, but never, shouted?

'I am not being cold,' Rafael said with exaggerated patience. 'I am simply trying to take the temperature down a notch or two. Getting worked up doesn't get anyone anywhere.'

'Oh, sorry, I forgot. You don't do hysterics.'

'No. I don't.' Without warning, he swerved the

car off the main road and down one of the winding country lanes which they had not yet left behind. It would be a while before they hit the motorway system.

Cristina drew back into her chair, alarmed when he killed the engine, unclasped his seat belt and then swung his body around so that he was facing her.

'What are you doing?' she asked unsteadily.

'I'm having a conversation.'

'We can talk while you drive.' She looked away and chewed her lower lip until there was the metallic taste of blood on her tongue.

'We could,' Rafael agreed smoothly. 'But I prefer to see your face when you're calling me a monster.'

'I wasn't calling you a monster.'

'Weren't you? You accuse me of doing you the disservice of asking you to be my wife because I think you would make a good wife—where is the insult in that?'

'I can't marry anyone for those reasons,' Cristina said, not looking at him. The view of fields and trees was a lot less threatening.

'You want me to tell you that I love you,'

Rafael ground out, and for a few seconds Cristina just wanted to cover his beautiful mouth with her hand, to stop that flow of words which she knew was coming. 'I cannot,' he said flatly. It was his turn now to feel outrage that she could have seen his generous offer as some kind of slap in the face. 'I've been down that road. I've told you that. Been down that road and seen for myself what lies at the end of it. So, no, love doesn't enter the equation.'

'But...' Cristina clung to those wonderful, tender memories of their love-making like a drowning person clasping a life belt, even though she could feel her fingers losing their grip as the waves continued to batter her.

'Yes, we made love.'

'Was that all part and parcel of the arrangement?'

'Don't be ridiculous.'

Here she was again, turned into a shrieking virago. *'I am not being ridiculous!'*

'I never realised that you possessed a voice that could shatter glass.'

'Nor did I!' But she drew in a few deep, steadying breaths. 'We made love...'

'And it was good.' His own voice dropped a

notch as he recalled their never-ending sessions between the sheets. Why the hell was she making this so difficult? She had been shocked at what she had interpreted as unromantic behaviour, but she would, he knew, get over that. She would come round to his point of view. He wondered whether to risk touching her, and decided that she would probably slap his hand away because she wasn't—as he was discovering—quite as meek and mild as he had imagined. 'Stop for a minute, Cristina, and think about what I'm saying. We're good together—good in bed…and out of it, come to that.'

'And so marrying me would make sense.' She felt jealousy claw at her when she thought of that other woman, the one into whom he had poured all his love, leaving him now without any to give anyone else. She had stolen his dreams and left him with a spreadsheet on which his future could be mapped out like figures in a profit-and-loss column. 'Rafael, the future isn't some kind of business deal that can be put together on a piece of paper. I won't sign my life away to someone because it seems to *make sense*. I would rather take my chances and wait for someone who might be able to give me the whole big thing.'

For a few unsettling seconds, Rafael wondered whether his smoothly made plans were in danger of being derailed. Having come this far in over-throwing his habits of a lifetime, in finally accepting the inescapable truth that he needed to settle down, he began to flounder at the preposterous notion that she might, really, be serious. Sure she had handed him back the ring, but women, he knew, were notorious for emotional outbursts later to be regretted.

'There *is* no such thing as *the whole big thing*,' he growled, uneasily aware that this was possibly not the right approach to be adopting in the face of mutiny.

'Maybe not for *you*,' Cristina snapped back, once again amazed at the shrew that seemed to have emerged from deep inside her. 'Or maybe you *had* your stab at the whole big thing and it didn't work out—but that doesn't mean that *I'm* prepared to give up my own dream on the back of the fact that *yours* fell flat!'

'You were happy enough to be my wife forty-eight hours ago,' Rafael told her, pointing out what he considered to be an inescapable truth. 'I'm finding it hard to understand what essentially has changed. I'm the same man I was then. Look at me!' he commanded. 'Have I suddenly turned into someone else? Morphed into an ogre? Grown an extra head? No.'

Cristina knew just how persuasive he could be when he put his mind to it. Whatever he wanted, he had once told her with a touch of satisfaction, he got. Simple as that. And sure, when he looked at her like this—covering her with his eyes, willing her to absorb what he was saying and yield to his greater wisdom—she could almost believe that he had a point, that love was just a word that was meaningless. Almost, but not quite.

'You don't understand,' she muttered.

'Then enlighten me.'

The silence stretched between them until he finally clicked his tongue impatiently. 'Okay—one. Do we have good times when we are together?'

'I guess.'

'You *guess*?'

'Okay, we do. Rafael, you can't sum things up like—'

'No. It's your turn to do the listening now. Two. Do I or do I not turn you on?'

'That's unfair. You know you do.'

'I know.' His mouth curled in sensuous satisfaction as his mind lingered on the very seductive image of her writhing under his exploring hands.

'Three. Would I or would I not make sure that your every material need was met?'

'You're asking the obvious.'

'That's what life is all about. The obvious. The minute we start layering it with shades of grey, we start getting caught in quicksand. Shall I tell you something very obvious?'

Cristina thought *no,* because nothing with Rafael was as obvious as he liked to pretend, least of all when he was attempting to appear as pure as the driven snow. She knew that verbally he could run rings around her, and that quicksand he had mentioned… Well, she would find herself well and truly drowning in it.

'What?' she heard herself saying.

'There's one place we haven't made love.'

The atmosphere was suddenly charged. From being on the defensive, Cristina could feel the drag of her senses pulling her under. His eyes were slumberous, and sent shivers racing impossibly through her body.

'You…you can't divert me with…by…'

'With…by…?' he mimicked, amused, back in control. 'Anyone would think that I had sent you into a tailspin.'

He reached forward and unclicked her seat belt, then he pushed it away, his arm brushing against her breast, making her gasp at the contact.

'*Now* tell me that this is a bad idea.' He leaned in towards her and crushed her open mouth under his, and Cristina's mind emptied of all thought as a blistering passion was unleashed. Hands that wanted desperately to push him away curled around his neck. She couldn't get enough of his kisses.

She had spent half the night berating herself for her foolishness in ever having got involved with him. She had given herself lecture upon lecture on the importance of love and the sanctity of marriage. In her head she had laughed derisively at him, and he had quailed at the logic of her arguments, admitting defeat and then begging her to be patient with him, to show him how to love. She had been the dominatrix cracking the whip, the bearer of truth and light, leading the way, fully in charge.

At no point in those imaginings had he scuppered proceedings by daring to touch her. Was that why she was now...*Lord, but no!*...allowing him to pull her across? To scramble until she was on his lap, where she could feel the pulsating of his stiffened member through the fine fabric of her summer dress?

She couldn't have chosen a more appropriate style for making love in a constricted space.

'I don't want this.'

Rafael held her face in both his hands, looked at her seriously, because forcing himself on a woman when she said no, even if her body said Yes, was not his style.

'You mean that?' he breathed huskily.

Cristina could feel herself drowning in his amazing eyes. Even when she blinked to clear her head, she still felt giddy.

'Yes. No. I don't know...'

'How can I change your mind?' Rafael asked softly, slipping his hand under the hemline of her dress which had ridden halfway up her thighs. He toyed provocatively with the lacy waistband of her underwear, running his finger along her stomach in a repetitive movement that was driving her crazy.

'I can't think when you're doing stuff like that.' Cristina heard the weak craving in her voice with despair, because there was still some small part of her brain functioning and it was telling her to stop this madness right now.

'Good,' Rafael encouraged soothingly. His finger dipped a little lower so that he could now feel the silkiness of her pubic hair, and just the tip of that crease which was teasing him with its promise of honeyed sweetness. 'Thinking can be a much overrated virtue,' he murmured. He slid his finger deeper and groaned as she squirmed against it.

'This is crazy.' Was it, though? Cristina now wondered. She felt confused, horrified at her inability to resist him—but pushing up behind those emotions was the thought that perhaps this was what she needed for closure. She needed to do this, to make love with him one last time. She couldn't go through her life haunted by the memory of his touch. She would be greedy and take this now. 'I mean,' she curved, pliant, against him. 'What if someone drives up this lane and sees us?'

Rafael breathed a sigh of relief. He wasn't sure what he would have done had she turned away from him. His body was on fire, as it always seemed to be when she was around, and in this neck of the woods passing motels with cold showers were few and far between.

'No one drives up these lanes,' he told her thickly, pushing his fingers deeper into that inviting cleft, and then cupping her with his hand. He could feel her dampness against his skin, an unbelievable turn-on. As was the knowledge that even in the midst of her rant she still couldn't resist him, still couldn't deny the demands of her own body.

He suddenly felt on top of the world.

Her dress was front-opening via a series of tiny, fiddly imitation-pearl buttons. Even though he felt on the verge of exploding, wanted to rip them apart, Rafael was going to take his time.

'In that case, why are they here?'

'For randy teenagers like us who can't hold on any longer.' He shot her one of those crooked grins that made her toes curl. In truth, everywhere around them was deserted. In the distance, she could spot some cows relaxing in the shade of a copse of trees. It was idyllic.

He began undoing the tiny buttons one by one, savouring the sight of her creamy flesh as it was gradually exposed to his hungry eyes.

Her lace bra was a flimsy barrier for her breasts. Through the white lace, her pink nipples peeped at him, making his taste buds go into immediate overdrive.

The Bentley, which was a comfortable ride, was now revealing the additional and unadvertised bonus of being incredibly spacious when it came to situations like this, especially for someone of his powerful build. He would definitely have to bear that in mind when they next took a drive through the countryside. Forget the Ferrari. Bring the Bentley.

Her dress was now opened to the waist, but instead of pulling it down, Rafael reached behind and expertly unclasped her bra, and as it loosened he pushed it up so that her heavy breasts spilled free.

The unease which he had earlier felt, when she had removed the engagement ring and given him her moralistic speech about love and romance, had disappeared.

He sighed and leaned forward so that he could lose himself in her.

Cristina watched his beautiful dark head descend and closed her eyes, arching back so that she could present her breasts to him. He adored them. Of that there was little doubt, and she would enjoy his adoration, even if it was only of her body, the least important part of her as far as she was concerned.

As he suckled on them, she felt that familiar fire course through her body, igniting those wanton urges which he had discovered and made his own.

She clasped her fingers into his hair and once more closed her eyes, sighing with a mixture of regret and pleasure as he continued to feast on her breasts, only finally surfacing when he couldn't, he confessed, hold back anymore.

'This is what you do to me,' he murmured roughly, as always slightly shaken by her ability to completely wipe out all his self-control.

She levered herself up as he jerkily unzipped his trousers. She, too, was on the point of no return. Watching him lavish attention on her was almost as erotic as the actual physical touch. For a man who could be arrogant, frighteningly self-assured and sometimes just plain exasperating in his need to control his surroundings, he was vulnerable in his desire.

The front windows had been rolled down, and a balmy breeze brought with it the distant sound of cows lowing and, from somewhere far away, a tractor turning over the fields.

Cristina, carried away on the wings of powerful, drugging passion, couldn't imagine ever doing this with anyone else. There were a lot of things she couldn't imagine doing with anyone else, but she closed her mind to all of that. And as their bodies joined, and she felt him thrust in her, she succumbed to those racing heights of pleasure that had her gasping and moaning and shuddering against him.

After a timeless period, they surfaced and their eyes met, Rafael's slumberous with satisfaction, Cristina's, if not with regret, then certainly with sadness.

She edged off him and did her best to straighten herself up in the confines of the car. She pulled down her bra, ignoring his lazy request that she remove it and shove it in the glove compartment.

'I mean,' he commented thoughtfully, 'We still have quite a distance to go. What if we decide that we need to take another break?'

'We won't.' She finished fastening the last of the pearl buttons. When she got back to her apartment, she would have the dress laundered and put away. Somewhere out of sight and out of reach, but still accessible should she ever want to take it out of its wrapping and remember.

She made a point of yawning and rested her head against the window.

Rafael was more than happy to let her sleep. Frankly, at this point in time, he was more than happy to let her do anything. That silly disagreement had been sorted in the most effective way possible. As he manoeuvred the Bentley back onto the main road, he glanced across and saw that she appeared, indeed, to have dozed off. She had forgotten to slip the engagement ring back on, but she would when they were back in London and maybe—who knew?—he might even talk to her about a country house. Not, naturally, as their main property, but something of a bolt hole. He knew that she had fabricated that whole nonsense about wanting to set up premises out of London—a fairy story to try and sow seeds of a possible cause for break-up in his mother's head—but there was probably something of a grain of truth there. She was not the sort of girl who belonged in the urban jungle.

The car ate up the miles back to London, and it was only when they slowed up to accommodate the weight of Sunday evening traffic getting into the city that Cristina opened her eyes, surprised that she had actually managed to nod off after all.

She must have been more tired than she had imagined, because closing her eyes had been the only ploy she could think of to avoid talking to Rafael. She didn't regret making love with him one last time, but she knew that the next conversation she would have with him was not going to be a comfortable one. He was in a buoyant frame of mind; one quick glance at his contented profile confirmed that, as did the jazz CD playing softly in the background. When he felt relaxed and happy, he had once confided to her, he liked to listen to music, and jazz music at those times was his preferred favourite.

'You're awake,' Rafael said, surprising her because she hadn't even been aware that he was looking at her. He looked across at her and his lips curved into a smile of pure sensuality. It was enough to make any woman do that impossibly Victorian thing of swooning.

'How much longer before I'm home?' was her response, and Rafael frowned, momentarily taken aback by a certain coolness in her voice. Immediately and generously, however, he put that down to simply waking up in a grumpy mood.

'Half an hour at the most,' he said. 'But why don't you come back to my place? We can carry on where we left off earlier…' Just the thought of that was enough to put a smile on his face.

Cristina watched that sexy smile, and felt a sinking despair inside her. She had to remind herself that she was doing the right thing. It wasn't even just that marriage, for her, was so much more than a *sensible* conclusion. There was also that niggling suspicion that if he didn't love her, if he could *never* love her, then what would happen when the lust tapered off? Would he begin to regret his decision? Worse, would he seek entertainment elsewhere? Would he justify infidelity by telling himself that he had never promised her love, that his bargain had been to take care of her, provide for her and the children which he had already mentioned he wanted, and nothing else? He was very hot on making sure that no woman he dated ever got the wrong message. That way, she later thought, he could break their hearts without compunction.

'I don't think that would be a very good idea, Rafael,' she murmured unhappily.

'Don't tell me that you're going to start back on that bandwagon?' he said tensely. He put his foot on the accelerator, switched off the music, which was now getting on his nerves, and stared ahead, swerving down a side road to escape the build up of traffic. 'I thought all that had been sorted out!'

'You mean because we had sex in your car?'

'Don't be crude.'

'I'm not being crude. I'm being honest.'

For the second time, Rafael felt himself back on the treadmill, walking fast but going nowhere. This time, though, he wasn't going to argue the toss. There was only so much any reasonable man, such as himself, was prepared to take. He had already argued his case and he wasn't going to treat her to a repeat performance. He told himself that, suitable though she was for the role of his wife, there were plenty more fish in the sea. His mother would, naturally, be disappointed. She had taken an instant liking to Cristina, but then again his mother would not be the other half of the partnership.

He also told himself that it would be futile hitching his wagon to a woman who wanted declarations of love. It wouldn't be long before the demands would begin—the complaints that he wasn't attentive enough, the petulance and sulks. He thought of his ex-wife. Well, Cristina probably wouldn't go down the road of throwing money down the drain on expensive trinkets, but who knew whether or not the infidelity would set in?

'Fine.' He shrugged in casual dismissal. Her distinguished converted Georgian house was now in view, and he turned down the wide, elegant street to pull up directly in front of her block.

'Fine?'

'Look, I've told you the parameters of this whole arrangement. If you can't accept it, then you can't accept it. You're right. If you want to chance your future on a man who can promise you everything you want, then feel free to pursue the dream. As you pointed out, it's no good being tainted by my take on marriage.' Rafael grimly wondered what sort of man she had in mind to fill the woolly, candy-floss fantasies in her head. Some limp-wristed nerd who would help her arrange flowers in her shop and promise her happy endings that would never materialise?

'However—' he gave her a lazy, assessing look '—it's going be tough finding Mr Right when you're in love with me, isn't it?'

Cristina felt her whole body begin to burn as those amazing eyes bored into her, making a mockery of feelings that she held precious, she thought. He was beyond cynical. Was that why he had pursued her with such confidence, had felt so guaranteed of success? She had been careful not to mention the 'love' word, but of *course* he would have known how she felt!

She wondered whether it had turned him on, knowing how powerful the effect he had on her was. Hadn't she read somewhere that that was sometimes how it worked? You could physically be attracted to someone, at least for a while, not because they were *your type,* but because they were so mad—keen on you that it was *an irresistible tug on the ego*. Of course, after a while, it just became boring.

She belatedly wished to high heaven that she hadn't exchanged experience for magazine articles.

'No.' She held her head high. 'Why should it?' Good question indeed, and he looked very interested in hearing what she had to say by way of response. She could have hit him! She actually could have resorted to physical violence and swung her handbag at him, wiped that smug half-smile off his face.

She scrabbled around to think of a suitably cutting reply, which was something of a struggle, because cutting replies didn't come easy to her. Eventually she said, frowning into the distance, 'I fell in love with a man who isn't capable of loving me back. Next time, I'll choose carefully. I'll go for the guy who wants to put *me* first, someone who doesn't think that marriage is some kind of maths equation that can be solved on a piece of paper, someone who isn't scared of emotional commitment, someone who—'

'I get the message,' Rafael cut in, the faintest tinge of colour darkening his aristocratic cheek-bones. 'And where do you think this paragon of saintliness is going to reside—aside from in your own imagination, of course?'

Cristina was finding it difficult to believe that this was the same man who had taken her breath away. 'I really feel sorry for you, Rafael,' she said with heartfelt sincerity. She opened the car door, ready to flee to the soothing calm of her little apartment.

'And that would be because…?' Why the heck was he feeling that he was losing the battle even though he was winning the war?

'Because…' she looked back over her shoulder '…what dreams do you have left if you don't dream of love and happiness? That's the one thing all the money in the world can't buy.'

CHAPTER EIGHT

Six weeks later, and that parting shot could still make Rafael scowl when he thought about it.

Fortunately for him, he had dusted himself off that whole sorry business with, he liked to think, the ease born of experience. In fact, as he looked across the dinner table at the sexy blonde sitting opposite him, he couldn't help but smile to himself and wonder whether Cristina was enjoying a similarly happy situation. Or was she, as he liked to imagine, curled up on that squashy patterned sofa in her apartment with a hot cup of cocoa and only her moral high ground for company?

'Share the joke with me?'

Rafael snapped out of that pleasant train of thought and focused on Cindy. Long-limbed, long-haired, full-lipped Cindy, all the way from America and every inch the advertising executive. She worked for a small but very upwardly mobile company which was now beginning to expand globally, and Rafael had met her at one of the many social events which he had crammed into the past few weeks, ever since the end of his relationship with Cristina. Initially he had found the constant round of parties, openings, dinners and theatre evenings a nightmare of boredom, but he had forced himself to attend them because, as far as he was concerned, he had become lazy in Cristina's company. He'd been happy to do very little including—and he shuddered to think about it—sitting in front of the television and indulging her passion for certain soap operas.

'I always smile when I find myself sitting opposite a beautiful woman,' Rafael said smoothly. 'You haven't eaten your fish. No good?'

'A girl has to…' Cindy patted her non-existent stomach and smiled ruefully. 'You know, watch her calorie intake, especially in my job. You'll never believe this, Rafael, but…' She leaned forward and whispered in a shocked undertone, 'Anyone even a *teeny weeny* bit overweight never gets through to the second round of interviews! You must *never* repeat that! But it's more or less a given.'

Rafael grunted something. He was in danger of losing interest, even though Cindy was very perky and very, very sexy. 'I'm thinking of having a party next weekend.' He changed the subject. 'My secretary's idea. Some important Japanese clients are coming over and she's suggested an informal affair at my place. Some pretty influential people will be invited.' He leaned across the table and took one of those long, elegant fingers in his. 'Care to come?' He had been seeing Cindy now for a fortnight and he had yet to invite her to his place. He also had yet to sleep with her, but his timetable had been frantic and this was, in actual fact, only the second time they had sat down together.

Her eyes lit up and she produced a thousand-watt smile from somewhere. 'I'd love to!' she squealed. It was, he thought, a predictable reaction. 'What shall I wear, hmm…?'

With admirable self-absorption and a running commentary on how important it was to dress for the part—because, wherever she was, she was always representing her company—Cindy lost herself in pleasant contemplation of the prospect, leaving Rafael time to muse on another dawning idea. A very good idea, as a matter of fact.

He thought of Cristina and her hot cup of cocoa. His mother had been shocked and disappointed at the outcome of their relationship. In fact, for reasons quite beyond him, she had jumped to the conclusion that it had all been his fault—a misunderstanding Rafael had not hastened to remedy, because a complicated story of Cristina and her childish nonsense about not wanting to marry anyone who didn't spout rubbish about undying love would have upset Maria. Worse, it would have incited lengthy and endless sermons on the topic of his cynicism, which was a trait his mother had never found particularly endearing.

She would heartily approve of him doing the decent thing and inviting his ex to his party. Taking her under his wing, so to speak, for all the right reasons. He had moved on with his life. Wouldn't it be the generous thing to do to make sure that Cristina wasn't heading for some kind of depression? He hadn't heard a word from her since she had flounced out of his car, pink faced and self-righteous, and trying to get information from his mother had been the equivalent of hitting his head on a brick wall.

He had even debated getting in touch with *her* parents in Italy, just to make sure that the woman hadn't done something incredibly silly. But then he had reminded himself, with a generous helping of that cynicism his mother so detested, that the only incredibly silly thing Cristina was likely to do would be to waste away her life in search of the non-existent.

'Are *you* going to be involved in the arrangements?'

Rafael surfaced and looked blankly at his date for a few seconds. Then he was back to reality, smiling and assuring her that he would naturally be taking no part in arranging anything.

'Why should you?' Cindy asked, her green eyes lingering seductively on his face. 'You're an important man. Why not let someone else do all the boring stuff?'

'Why not indeed?' Rafael murmured. He knew when his ego was being stroked and it was being stroked now. He also knew when a woman's eyes were lingering on him with one thing in mind. He looked at his watch and then regretfully signalled for the bill. 'Afraid I'm going to have to let you get your beauty sleep tonight,' he told her without preamble. 'I'm on a plane to Australia first thing in the morning, and I have a thousand emails to get through before my head hits the pillow.'

More or less the truth, but if his libido was anything to go by he was really more tired than he'd thought; even that kiss on the lips, which should have had him dismissing his driver and following her into her flat in Battersea, barely got his pulses racing.

'I'll be in touch,' he promised, guiltily aware that she wanted a hell of a lot more than he was in the mood to give. 'I'm going to get my secretary onto this whole party thing and I'll let you know the details.' With the engine running and his driver waiting, Rafael kissed her again, this time with slightly more vigour. But when she would have pulled him closer towards her so that she could press her amazing but surgically enhanced breasts against his chest, he pulled away, gently loosening her hands from his neck.

'Get something for yourself to wear from Harrods,' he said, vaguely aware that this was meagre compensation for leaving her on a Saturday night on her own, when she had clearly been offering her company into the early hours of the morning. 'Just tell them to put it on my account. I'll make sure my secretary clears it.'

That, at least, did the trick. Cindy's face, on the verge of a pout, broke into a radiant smile.

'Are you sure about that?'

Relieved to be off the hook, Rafael nodded and took a step back. 'Whatever you want,' he told her. 'I want you looking… Well, let's just say you won't have to try very hard.'

'But I'll still enjoy it, especially when I know that you'll be waiting to see what's under the sexy clothes as soon as the last person leaves…'

She drew her finger tantalisingly along her exposed cleavage and shot him a slow, coy smile. Rafael could well imagine that a thousand men would have melted from the heat of that smile, but his head was already racing away to the emails he had to send, and to a certain call he would make as soon as he got back to his apartment.

He nodded his head, appreciating her with his eyes, but relieved that his driver gave him the excuse to beat a retreat. His attention was firmly elsewhere by the time he was finally back in his apartment and switching on the lights.

He poured himself a glass of mineral water,

looked at the computer waiting for him on the kitchen counter, where he had left it charging in his absence, and grabbed the phone from its handset.

He had almost near-perfect recall, and jabbed in Cristina's number as he stretched out on the long sofa in the living room. Of course she would be in. Not for a minute did he contemplate the possibility that at ten-thirty on a Saturday evening she might be out doing the London scene.

She might have waxed lyrical about Mr Right, but hunting him down would have been a completely different matter. She wasn't a hunter. She was utterly, maddeningly feminine and would have been appalled at the concept of getting out there and being proactive.

Sure enough, it was a drowsy voice that answered after just three rings.

'Have I woken you up?' Rafael demanded, disregarding all rules of basic politeness.

'Rafael?'

'Well? Were you asleep?'

The sound of that dark, velvety and supremely arrogant voice was like a bucket of ice-cold water being thrown over her head.

For the past six weeks she had tried really hard

to get him out of her head, and she had managed to convince herself that it was working. She had applied to start a formal evening-course in landscape gardening, and had been ploughing through a mountain of books in preparation. In between her daily running of the flower shop, it had just about been enough to see her through those nasty times when memories of him would pounce, like a monster let out of a cupboard, pummelling her hard-fought good intentions.

For Anthea's sake she had also tried to put a brave face on things, had shrugged off the cancelled engagement as 'one of those things', as though broken engagements were a daily occurrence in her life, and had been as bright and breezy as she could.

She had, however, drawn the line at launching herself into the single life, despite her friend's attempts to get her out there in the social scene.

Hearing Rafael's voice now catapulted her straight back in time. Her small hard-won achievements evaporated and she sat up in bed, every nerve in her body tensing.

'What do you want?' she asked tightly, and down the end of the line she heard him sigh.

Well, she hadn't *asked* him to call her, hadn't heard a word from him for weeks, so why was he sighing as though *she* had been the one to interrupt him in the middle of his super-busy life? Immediately she thought that Rafael would not have seen things that way and she was so guiltily, stupidly pleased to hear his voice that she fell silent.

'There's no need to snap,' Rafael said silkily. 'I mean, I'm not interrupting anything, am I?'

Cristina dearly wished that she could answer that in the affirmative. But her evening had been spent watching a gardening show on television, having something of a comfort-eating fest on her own and spending half an hour on the phone to her mother who had taken to calling her every couple of days to *cheer her up*.

'No,' she admitted reluctantly, 'Not really. Why are you calling? What do you want?'

What Rafael really wanted was to tell her that he could actually have been in the company of a stunningly beautiful blonde who would never have dreamed of speaking to him as though he were something that had crawled out from under a rock—but in time he remembered that she was probably still angry and bitter with him.

'I wanted to find out how you were.' He relaxed, resting his arm under his head and loosely linking his feet at the ankles where he stared down at his black socks, having previously kicked off his shoes by the front door.

'I'm very well, thank you.'

'Good. I'm glad to hear it. I was worried about you.' His voice bordered on pious.

'Well, I don't believe that for a minute, Rafael. And you still haven't told me why you're calling me at this hour.'

'Most of London are up at *this hour*,' he pointed out. 'And I was calling to invite you out.'

On a date? was the wild thought that flew through her head. Then she remembered what he was all about. He was the man who had a stone for a heart even if he did manage to give a very good impression of a living, breathing, *normal* human being.

'I don't think so.' She remembered the way they had laughed together, the way he had indulged her inclination to babble, the way he had made her feel sexy and good about herself.

Very firmly, she shut the door on those nagging, enticing memories.

'To a party I'm having next weekend at my place here in London.'

'You want to invite me to a party…?' That was more like it. He wasn't really interested in finding out about *her* and how *she* was doing; he probably felt bad because he had hurt her. Not, obviously, so bad that he wanted to check on her welfare face to face over a cup of coffee, but bad enough to consider asking her along to something large and impersonal which would give him the opportunity to ask a few polite questions with the comfort of having a crowd of his friends around. Just in case she started blubbing or something. She wondered whether his mother had put him up to it.

'Hello? Are you still there? Or have you dozed off in mid-thought?'

'Of course I haven't *dozed off*!' Cristina snapped. 'See? You've only been on the phone for two seconds and already you're making me shout!'

'There's nothing wrong with emotional responses.'

'That's not what you've said in the past,' Cristina reminded him sourly.

That, Rafael had to concede to himself, had a ring of truth about it.

'Well?' he demanded. 'Can I count you in or not?'

'Why have you asked me? Do you feel sorry for me? Did Maria put you up to it?'

'No one has put me up to anything, in answer to your first question. And in answer to your second… Is there any reason why I should feel sorry for you? I mean, life moves on, doesn't it?' He tried to visualise Cindy's face in his head, but instead a very clear image of Cristina's rose to the forefront.

So he *did* feel sorry for her. His non-answer was as good as a positive response and, while Cristina didn't want to go to any party he might be having—didn't want to be in his presence at all, not when she was obviously still so vulnerable to his overpowering personality, even when she was just receiving it via radio waves at the end of a telephone—well, to refuse would be to admit that she just couldn't face him. He would feel even sorrier for her then!

As if tuning in to her innermost thoughts and

reading her mind, Rafael drawled, 'You're not scared of seeing me, are you?'

Cristina forced herself to relax by breathing slowly and deeply—another piece of received wisdom from one of the many magazines she had devoured as a youth when she should have been out there gaining valuable experience with boys, as all her friends had been doing.

'Don't be silly. Why should I be scared of seeing you?'

'I'll let you know more details closer to the day.'

'I thought you said that it was going to be next weekend?' Cristina found herself distracted by his vagueness. 'Haven't you arranged it as yet?'

'Oh, I won't have a hand in that. Patricia's going to take care of the whole thing.'

Typical, she thought. Not for a single second would it have occurred to him that last-minute affairs stood a greater than average chance of being flops. How many people were available at such short notice? But of course, this was Rafael Rocchi, the man for whom people jumped through hoops.

'I take it from your silence that you don't approve of my lack of involvement?'

'You can take it from my silence that I'm not surprised at your lack of involvement. I'll have to look in my diary and see what I'm doing next weekend,' she said, buying herself time, because she honestly wasn't sure whether she could face him or not.

'Good. I'll see you then. And Cristina…?'

'What.'

'Feel free to bring a date.'

Those were the words, spoken with lazy amusement, that galvanised her into a positive decision. Cristina knew that she didn't have to prove anything to anyone, but she really needed to start getting her life back together. She had done the right thing in standing up for herself, for holding on to her dreams of a happy marriage with the right guy who could love her back—but what was the point of doing the right thing if she then proceeded to spend the rest of her days moping around and thinking about Rafael?

She had turned down all of Anthea's well-intentioned invitations to go out, had buried herself in indoor pursuits, had assured her mother and her sisters that she was doing just fine, when in fact she had spent the past few weeks hiding out in her apartment as if scared to venture outside in case she collapsed. Why should she collapse? From the sounds of it, Rafael was as chirpy as a cricket and getting on with his life, and she wasn't going to let him join the queue of people silently feeling sorry for her.

Anthea, of course, was overjoyed.

'It'll do you the world of good to get out,' she said firmly. 'And you can show him that you've moved on. Maybe you could ask Martin to go along with you? Sort of *borrow* him for the evening?'

Tempting though the thought was, Cristina baulked at the thought of such an obvious piece of deception. She liked Martin a lot as a friend, but she wasn't going to use him as a pretend trophy-boyfriend just to prove a point.

But she did allow herself to get swept into shopping for an outfit, something new and colourful to reflect her new and colourful life. Privately, Cristina thought that the description made her sound as though she had taken up pole-dancing in a nightclub. But she was happy to let Anthea steer her in and out of shops until, by the end of the week, she had accumulated one dress, way too short, one pair of shoes, way too high, and various assorted bits of costume jewellery which would have sent her father into an early grave had he clapped eyes on them.

'And I'll be round at six on Saturday to fix you up!' Anthea told her. 'You're going to be the belle of the ball!'

Cristina was far from sure about that. The dress was a vibrant deep red with a neckline that went beyond plunge into full-blown dive, but her breasts, her friend had declared, were her assets and should be displayed with pride. And no, she wouldn't fall face-first in front of the assembled crowd in her high heels. She would walk in a sexy but dignified manner and all eyes would be on her. Cristina accepted those words of wisdom with a little sigh of resignation.

Rafael's secretary, when she had called earlier in the week with details of the evening, had offered to send his driver round to collect her, but Cristina had refused, preferring to make her own way there by taxi. And it was just as well, because Anthea was late in arriving and, by the time she had been 'fixed up', she was already running behind time.

But she did, she had to admit, look glamorous. The dress, which had looked idiotic in the changing room when tried on with her trainers, did all the right things. It accentuated her bust, nipped in her waist, and her legs looked much longer than they really were in the shiny, patent-black high heels.

They had bought loads of costume jewellery, which jangled around her neck down to her waist, and Anthea had done clever things with her hair, pinning it up but very casually so that it tumbled around her face and made her eyes look sultry and enormous. She had managed to argue her way out of vast amounts of make-up, but her lips were still red, and the faint blush on her cheeks highlighted cheekbones which she had never known really existed.

All told, Cristina was confident that she at least looked her best, even if inside she felt far from it.

The flutter of nerves which had begun the minute she had accepted the invitation were in full force by the time the taxi dropped her outside his place.

Patricia had said that it would be a small, quiet gathering, really in honour of their Japanese clients with whom they had recently closed a major deal.

Standing outside his door, it sounded neither small nor quiet. She was discreetly pressing her ear against the door, anxiously chewing her lower lip and wondering whether she could sneak back out and escape under cover of gathering darkness, when the door was pulled open and there he was. Tall, darkly, fatally handsome and waiting to catch her as she stumbled against him.

Cristina hurriedly gathered herself, flustered.

'What are you doing?' Rafael asked, as taken aback to see her standing there as she was to find the door opened when she had been pressed against it.

He wasn't quite sure what had brought him to the door. At the back of his mind, with the party in full swing and Cindy playing the perfect hostess, much to his annoyance he had been waiting for Cristina to arrive. She was one of the most punctual women he had ever met and he knew that after an hour he had been glancing at his watch every three minutes, his mind only half on what was happening around him.

He hadn't expected to open his door to find her toppling against him.

Nor had he expected her to be wearing what she was wearing.

He held her at arm's length and looked at her appraisingly.

'You said it was a party,' Cristina said defensively before he could say anything. 'So I dressed for a party.'

'So I see.' His hands appeared to be temporarily glued to her arms and he quickly removed them. 'I'm not sure I would call this strip of red cloth a *dress*.' He had wondered how she was, had thought about her far too much for his liking, had assumed that she was missing him. In fact he had been worried enough about her well-being, and *caring* enough to invite her to his party, magnanimous as he was.

From the looks of things, he had been way off target. He had never seen her in a get-up like this before. She looked… sexy as hell and *ready for anything*.

An imagination which he'd never known he possessed suddenly slammed into action, and he had vivid images of her dealing with her loss in the classic way. He pictured her going out on the town, meeting strange men in strange bars. God.

When he had called her the week before and imagined that he had caught her sleeping in on a Saturday night, she had probably been in bed all right. But not alone.

'You're barely decent!' He found himself positioning himself directly in front of her, blocking her from the crowd of people milling around inside.

Having left all arrangements in the capable hands of his secretary, the party of twenty people had somehow turned into a lavish affair with more than forty people, who had been steadily getting tipsy on the champagne and Chablis from the moment of their arrival well over an hour ago. The waiters were assiduous in their duties, never allowing a glass to remain empty for longer than five seconds, it seemed, and the array of delicious and abundant canapés were doing the rounds, but were hardly robust enough to mop up the quantity of alcohol on offer. Rafael had no doubt that he would have to send out for something more substantial on the food front at some point, but at the moment…

He shuffled so that he could now half shut the door behind him.

His movements didn't go unnoticed and Cristina, who had left her house feeling a million dollars, now wanted to tug the dress down and stick her little clutch bag in front of her breasts. Was he embarrassed at her? Did he think that her outfit was going to lower the tone of his party?

Nothing like this had ever happened to her before, and she was mortified to think that it could be happening now.

'If you'd rather I left…' She risked a quick, desperate glance over her shoulder.

'Of course not. You're here now. I'm just surprised at your choice of clothing.'

'Anthea gave me a hand,' Cristina confessed.

'Right.' Rafael wondered what else Anthea had done to *give her a hand* since they had broken up. Taken her to a few rave parties, maybe? Dressed like that, there wasn't a man in London who wouldn't have done a double take.

'Well…shall we go inside?'

'Of course!' He stood back and watched grimly as she entered the room and, as he'd expected, the red dress—or rather the lack of it, in combination with her all too obvious womanly charms—had every man in the room covertly looking in her direction. And naturally Cindy, whose eyes narrowed as she strolled over slowly, but very purposefully, in their direction.

She had dressed to impress and had toed a fine line between sexy and 'blonde but wanting to be taken seriously'. Consequently, she had ended up looking somewhat like a very attractive, super-efficient air stewardess, in a dove-grey skirt with small matching jacket, grey shoes and a white blouse with a couple of buttons discreetly left undone. Next to Cristina, she was a pale shadow of a woman, but he still smiled winningly in her direction and slung his arm casually around her shoulders as she nestled against him and gave Cristina a very thorough once-over.

'Welcome to our little gathering,' Cindy said. She gave Rafael a little squeeze that was clear indication to Cristina that he really and truly had moved on. Moved on to a gorgeous, leggy blonde who wasn't dressed like a clown. Cristina wanted the ground to open and swallow her up, but she smiled brightly, because there was no law against Rafael finding happiness with someone else even if it was like a dagger through her heart.

The waiter came round with a tray of drinks

and Cristina hurriedly grabbed one, making up her mind there and then that she would need a couple of drinks to see the evening through.

Cindy, all smiles and elegance, was now taking charge, shooing Rafael away to his guests and assuring him that she would take little Cristina under her wing, make sure that she was introduced to some interesting *young* people.

Cristina gulped down what was left of the wine in her glass and tried not to feel like a kid in fancy dress at an adult gathering.

After three glasses of Chablis and no nibbles, because she felt fat, the party was taking on a much more agreeable tenor. For a start, Rafael might have thought that she looked cheap and tarty, but several of the *young* men there appeared to be of a different opinion. In fact, several of the *more mature* men seemed to share the feeling.

By the time she happened to glance at her watch it was after midnight and she had, she thought, done rather well. She had kept a healthy distance from Rafael—not wanting to be reminded of his newly evolved state with the glamorous and very solicitous Cindy—and she had, in addition, gathered a few very useful numbers from people who were interested in talking to her about her landscaping plans.

Indeed, one was, at this very moment, in the process of persuading her that he was in desperate need of her talents.

'But I thought you lived in an apartment,' she pointed out gently.

'I do, and you need to get over there and have a look. My potted plants are in dire need of some love and attention…'

'You're drunk, Goodman. Time to go. I've called a cab and it's waiting.'

Cristina, who had been enjoying the flattery and wondering if she shouldn't be asserting her joy of singledom by accepting his invitation to view his boxed plants, swung round at the sound of Rafael's voice.

The room had emptied. How and when had that happened? She looked around in panic for her forgotten clutch bag, but by the time she had visually located it Rafael was back, standing in front of her, arms folded, his face grim.

'I'll just be on my way,' she said, backing away in the direction of the bag. 'I had no idea everyone had disappeared!' She gave a nervous little giggle.

'No, I don't suppose you did,' Rafael grated. 'You were so absorbed in the charms of James Goodman that the proverbial sky could have fallen down and you wouldn't have noticed.' The night, as far as Rafael was concerned, had been a disaster. The guests had bored him after half an hour, Cindy had been appalling in her desperation to prove her hostess abilities and stake her claim—and Cristina, whom he had imagined might come and shyly hang back, compelling him to draw her out, had stolen the show. He had no intention of telling her, but several people had asked about her, wondered who she was. The whole experience had not been a good one, and now here she was, eager to scuttle off, probably in the hope of catching Goodman before he left the scene of the crime.

'Where's…um…Cindy?' she asked, in the face of his stony silence. 'She seems a very nice woman…'

Rafael was in no mood to think about Cindy, whom he had dispatched twenty minutes earlier in a move that would certainly herald the demise of any fledgling relationship. He wasn't too concerned. If after having met her only a couple of times he had found her company grating, then it was clearly doomed.

'I could warn you that, if this is your way of handling our break up, then you're heading for an almighty fall, but…' He shrugged elegantly. 'It's entirely up to you how you behave in public…'

'How I *behave in public*?' Cristina said, with mounting anger at his attitude. He seemed to think that it was perfectly fine to spend the evening with a six-foot blonde draped over him like ivy—but *she*, on the other hand, had arrived dressed indecently and now, from what he was saying, had made a fool of herself. She tried to count to ten but only managed to make it to three, then she placed her hands squarely on her hips and glared ferociously at him.

'I'm free, young, single, and…and…' *And what?* 'And looking for fun! Yes, I might be dressed in a short skirt…'

'With every inch of your body on display.' Rafael interposed tightly.

'But you've taught me how to get out there and face the world!'

'So now it's *my* fault that you're now prowling for men?'

Cristina thought of her nights in with cocoa and gardening books and decided not to correct him. How dared he? *When he had already replaced her?*

'I don't have to *prowl for men*!' she said, thinking on her feet and for once coming up with a stinging riposte. 'I've noticed that a fair number of them find me quite attractive! In fact…' She walked quickly towards her clutch bag and pulled out a little wad of telephone numbers. There was no way that she was going to tell him that most of them were genuine enquiries about her landscaping services from some of the wives who had been there.

'Look—numbers! *Telephone numbers!* Including Jamie's! And, yes, I won't be *sitting around waiting for them to call me!*'

CHAPTER NINE

RAFAEL'S week had not gone well. He had wasted a great deal of time reliving his party, and had been inconveniently plagued with thoughts of Cristina in her sexy and—as he liked to mentally describe it—tarty outfit. *Out there looking for fun.*

He had felt sorry for her, gentleman that he was, had invited her because he had wanted to make sure that she was doing okay. She was, he had been forced to concede to himself, doing more than okay. She was, judging from the looks of it, painting the town red.

He had also had a couple of very uncomfortable conversations with Cindy, who had mistakenly interpreted three dates as the wheels beginning to turn on a bandwagon of 'getting to know one another'. He hadn't wanted to retaliate in any way to her accusations of being used, but in the end had been forced to tell her that they simply weren't compatible. Instead of being consoled by that suitably vague excuse, she had begun to cry down the telephone and had launched into a really aggravating attack on him personally—at the end of which she had dared shout at him that he was just the sort of man her mother had always warned her about, after which she had slammed down the receiver.

Well, he could cope with that. Indeed, it had been a relief, because the whole business of going out with another woman, going through the getting-to-know-you routines which he had always rather enjoyed, had been giving him a headache. He could have been a bit more tactful, he supposed, in letting her know how he felt, but all that was in the past now.

No, that had been fine, but this…

He stared darkly at the phone on his desk, which he had only just replaced on its handset.

It was just as well that it was Friday, that he was the sole person left in the office—everyone else having virtually stampeded out of the building by the ridiculously early time of seven—because he was finding it difficult to focus after his conversation with Goodman.

He had hesitated before calling the man, but a couple of shared games of squash and the occasional work titbit tossed his way in the past had more than qualified him, in his eyes, for a surprise call. He had, naturally, sweetened things considerably by holding out the dazzling carrot of investing some money in the man's company. Not such a far-flung idea, as Rafael had been toying with extending his portfolio for a few months, and sure enough Goodman had leapt at the bait. It had taken only the tiniest strand of curiosity, thrown in virtually as an afterthought before ringing off, for Rafael to learn what he had wanted to know from the very beginning.

Namely whether Goodman had any intentions of seeing Cristina.

Rafael had not cared for the answer. The handkerchief-sized red dress which had accentuated all her natural assets, along with her *looking for fun* frame of mind, had worked its magic. A date, he had been informed with a disgusting amount of relish, was planned for later that evening. In fact, Goodman had practically crowed down the phone, he'd had to get his skates on if he was to meet her in time at the restaurant he had booked in the West End.

Rafael had received this information through gritted teeth, and had immediately taken precautionary action by telling him that he would have to cancel his hot date.

'Going to spring something on you, Goodman,' he had said, without a twinge of conscience. 'But my legal team have done rather more work on this particular investment than I originally let on, and if we're to move ahead we've got to do it quickly. I'm going to download an evening's worth of work…and I'll need your comments by tomorrow morning.' He had allowed sufficient time for his silence to be construed as rueful. Also for Goodman to appreciate just how much his firm would benefit from Rafael's much-needed injection of funds. He had added with killer instinct, ''Course, I have a number of companies I'm thinking of investing in…the opportunity would not be lost elsewhere…'

The conclusion to their conversation had been predictable: hot dates were good, but work came first.

Now, staring at the telephone as though at an

object capable of spreading contamination, Rafael tried and failed to put the whole thing out of his mind. He really would have liked to sweep the matter under the carpet, but he was realistic enough to realise that that just wasn't going to happen.

For some reason the woman had got under his skin and, even now, with their relationship dead and buried, she was still getting under his skin.

He thought of Goodman, eyes popping out, staring at her breasts, mentally calculating how long he could feasibly wait before he tried to get her into bed, and congratulated himself on taking the action that he had.

Without bothering to talk himself out of his decision, he grabbed his jacket and stuck it on while his computer was logging off, then he headed for the door.

This was unprecedented behaviour. He was fully aware of that, but all rational thought processes appeared to have disengaged and his feet had a game plan of their own, taking him down the stairs because the exercise was good, into the underground car park and towards the Ferrari which had been parked up for the past four days.

It started at the first attempt, and before he

could think through what he was doing he was on his way to her apartment.

The traffic, to his immense frustration, was atrocious. He hadn't noticed before, but London seemed to be awash with road works—and, he thought, scowling, even with a million red-and-white cones in place no one appeared to be working.

He had plenty of time to imagine what the course of her evening would have been like had he not ensured that it was stillborn. Drinks and dinner at Harvey Nicols, where the noise levels in the bar would have been loud, the service slow and the opportunities boundless for Goodman to make sure that she worked her way through a decent amount of alcohol before dinner. He couldn't imagine that it was her sort of place, but then neither could he have imagined her dressed in a red handkerchief and *looking for fun.*

It was well after eight by the time he had circled her road a couple of times and managed to find a spot to park.

At least he didn't have Goodman to worry about. He had picked up a message on his BlackBerry a couple of minutes earlier, assuring him that the caseload was being scanned even as he spoke.

He pressed her flat number and waited for her to pick up, which she did. Goodman would have told her by now that the date was off. He wondered whether another had been set. Maybe the man had intimated that he would drop by later for a nightcap.

'I was in the area,' Rafael said, 'So I thought I'd drop by.'

Cristina pulled back as if someone had suddenly shot a bolt of electricity through her body. James, her date, had called to say that he was in a bit of a pickle with work, and she had been guiltily aware of feeling a sense of relief. Having agreed to go out with him in the first place, she had spent the past two days having second thoughts.

He was an unashamed flirt. Without the safety net of a roomful of Rafael's friends and colleagues, she had been getting that 'out of her depth' feeling that had only increased a couple of notches when he had said, over the phone, that he would call her the following day because 'he couldn't wait to show her a good time'.

So Rafael's voice on her intercom, while a shock to the system, left her feeling a little giddy with relief. She had thought for a split second that James had decided to jettison the heavy workload and had somehow managed to get to her place so that he could show her this *good time* he had mentioned.

Not that she was going to give Rafael any inkling of what was going through her head. Not a chance. She had spent the past few days thinking about the new woman in his life, and telling herself that she needed to likewise move forward by having a chap on her arm. Or at least a possibility in her address book.

'Well? Are you going to open the door or not?'

'What are you doing here?' she said, stalling.

'I told you. I was in the area. Why not drop by? After all, we hardly spoke at the party.'

'Well, we did, actually,' Cristina was constrained to point out. 'When I arrived, you told me that I looked awful, so after that I thought it best to keep out of your way.'

'Open up the door. We can talk about this when I'm inside.'

Cristina chewed her lip, hesitating, and finally

she pressed the button to open the front door downstairs because she knew that he wasn't going to go away until he was allowed in. Besides, despite all the bracing lectures she'd given herself on a daily basis about the unfeeling, cold, sad human being that he was—a man she was well rid of—her unruly heart still wanted to lay into him for the speed with which he had moved on to another woman.

She still hadn't changed out of her going-out outfit. James had mentioned something about a smart restaurant in the West End and she had dressed accordingly, in an elegant turquoise dress that clung to the figure she was more proud now to have on display than ever before in her life.

On the verge of getting undressed and settling down for a night in watching television, she had kicked off the high shoes. Now she stuck them back on as she waited for Rafael to appear. Rafael was a dominating presence as it was without the added advantage of towering over her even more because she was barefoot.

She heard the rap on the door and momentarily froze, even though she had been waiting for that rap with every straining inch of her body.

She had to take a few deep breaths before pulling open the door. Normally that did the trick whenever she was nervous, but this time it had the opposite effect of making those somersaults in her stomach even more frantic.

She involuntarily stepped back the minute she saw him, and he immediately took advantage and brushed past her into the small hallway.

The previous Saturday, Rafael had looked devastatingly handsome at his party, but this was the look she had grown accustomed to and loved most: that end-of-day, slightly dishevelled look. His hair always looked as though he had been running his fingers through it, and he had seldom walked through her door in the evening without his sleeves cuffed to the elbows and his tie stuffed into his briefcase or in a pocket somewhere. At the start of the day he looked powerful, at the end of the day he looked downright dangerous.

'Going out?' Rafael asked, swinging round to look at her, perfectly aware that thanks to his intervention she would be going nowhere tonight.

She was wearing another dress which he hadn't seen before, another sexy number designed to show off her fabulous curves. For someone who had once preached the virtues of practical clothing, she seemed to have discovered the allure of the impractical wardrobe. First siren-red, now a turquoise that was exquisitely dramatic against her skin, and the way it clung… Having had an uninterested libido for the past few weeks, he now had the insane urge to strip her of her cling-film garment and take her the way he'd used to when things had been going good between them. Before she'd tried to pin him into a corner and turn him back into the kind of man who had seen his ex-wife grow bored and demanding and eventually unfaithful.

For a few seconds, Cristina was seriously tempted to lie and tell him that, yes, she was just about to leave her apartment, but then where would she go? She had no date, and there was no way that she was going to circle the block like a fugitive just to pretend that she was as busy on the romance front as he obviously was.

'I was,' she confessed stiffly. 'But something came up and my date had to cancel.'

'Nothing worse than an unreliable date,' Rafael purred smoothly, dragging his eyes off her and heading up the stairs so that she had no option but to follow him.

He was standing in front of the open fridge with a wine bottle in his hand by the time she joined him in the kitchen, and he took down a couple of wineglasses and placed them on the counter. 'So who was the lucky guy?' Rafael asked casually. 'Anyone I know?'

'James,' Cristina mumbled. 'Actually, I met him at your party last weekend.'

Rafael knitted his brows together in a frown and then raised his eyebrows in amused disbelief. 'Not Goodman.'

'As a matter of fact, yes.' She accepted the glass of wine and thought of the blonde at the party, at which point she tried to look suitably gutted that she wasn't going to be seeing James as planned.

There was a long and seemingly significant silence, and she reluctantly said, 'Why?' even though she could tell from that look on his face that that was precisely the question he had been waiting for.

'I thought that might be the case,' Rafael acknowledged, draining his glass and then leaning against the counter so that he could pin her down with his silvered gaze. 'Call it a gut feeling.'

'I have no idea what you're talking about.'

'I must have a highly developed telepathic side,' he mused. 'Because I got to thinking about you at the party, and I realised that I should probably come over and at least warn you that, if you're thinking of finding Mr Right in the shape of Goodman, then you're barking up the wrong tree.'

Cristina flushed and folded her arms. *Come over? Warn her?* Was she some sort of *charity case*? This confirmed everything she had been thinking. He had felt sorry for her and so had invited her to his little party, and he now not only felt sorry for her but he had also decided that she was somehow incapable of looking after herself.

'Did you *know* that James would get in touch with me?' she asked tightly.

Rafael was quick to deny any such thing. He suffered not the slightest tug of his conscience in doing so, because he could now see that she really was in need of his advice. He had tried to tell her that her suddenly revised dress code was not such a good idea, and as he could now see, she was in dire need of a few more words of caution.

'I use him as an example,' he said, oozing well-intentioned concern. 'He's typical of how a man will react in the presence of a woman who has her sexuality stamped all over her in neon lettering.'

Cristina was torn between feeling treacherously flattered that he'd thought her sexy and pure outrage that he'd had the cheek to swan over to her house to continue his silly preaching at her.

'I don't need you to give me a lecture on men,' she muttered, staring down at the pointed tips of her high-heeled shoes, very glad she had decided to stick them on—even though she could feel the beginnings of a blister on her right heel, and would have liked nothing more than to kick them off and slip into her comfortable bedroom slippers.

'Not if your intention is to work your way through a series of Mr Wrongs before you hit upon Mr Right.' He was in front of her practically before Cristina had time to raise startled eyes and take the necessary evasive action. Of course she should never have let him into her apartment, she had only herself to blame for the mortifying discomfort into which she was now plunged. But the minute Rafael spoke, every good-intentioned bone in her body turned to water. She had heard that deeply, sexy drawl at the end of the line and had melted.

'How can you preach to me about…about sleeping around?' she flung back at him defensively. 'You've already got someone else in your life! Or was that Cindy woman just a *good friend*?'

'We're not talking about me. I'm fully capable of handling myself.'

'I know that. It's the women you handle yourself with that are the ones in need of the sympathy vote.'

Why was she defending Goodman? Rafael thought savagely. She couldn't really believe that the man was anything but trouble as far as women were concerned? He was about to make that very point when he realised that she had lumped *him* into exactly the same category. It was a thought that was frankly outrageous, considering he had proposed marriage to her!

'Whatever impression you may have had,' he said, his brilliant eyes fixed on her downturned face, 'Cindy and I were never lovers.'

Cristina knew that it was foolish to be gladdened by that piece of information. It took nothing away from the fact that he had seen her as a convenience in his life rather than the driving love of it. They still stood at opposite sides of an unbreachable chasm. Nevertheless, she couldn't prevent a flood of pure happiness from pouring through her, and she decided that it was just nice to know that she hadn't been so instantly forgotten.

'Goodman has a reputation,' Rafael told her abruptly. 'And, yes, I know you're probably tarring me with the same brush, but you have yet to know James.'

'He seemed perfectly all right to me.' She raised her head and looked him straight in the eyes, which made it difficult for her to stay in control of her wits which he had an unnerving ability to scatter.

'If by "perfectly all right", you mean he spent the evening leering at your breasts…'

'I suppose now you're going to give me that talk about how unsuitable my dress was. I suppose you're going to tell me that what I'm wearing now is unsuitable as well…'

That focused Rafael's gaze exclusively on her body, which she was offering to his scrutiny, her hands hanging limply at her sides as she awaited the expected verdict.

Like an accumulated and unstoppable force, Rafael felt a charge of desire so powerful that he balled his hands into clenched fists in an attempt to control it. But his head was running wildly out of control, remembering the feel of her under his hands, and the taste of her as she'd writhed beneath him.

His nostrils flared and he heard himself asking, in a harsh undertone, 'Is this the first time you're seeing him this week? Did he touch you? Have you been to bed with him?' These were questions which in all fairness he couldn't ask the man himself, not without sounding like an enraged and jealous lover, but he found himself asking them now and hanging on for her response.

'Of course I haven't been to bed with him! When do you imagine that would have taken place? I only met him last weekend!'

'That says nothing,' Rafael dismissed scathingly.

'I'm not that type of girl. I thought you knew that much about me.'

'Look at you! I once imagined that you weren't the kind of girl who dressed to impress men, but I was wrong about that, so I can be wrong about everything else as well!'

'I'm not dressing to impress men!'

'Okay. Just Goodman.' He waited in the expectation that she would deny such a provocative accusation, and was even more furious when she failed to do so. If she had just accepted his marriage proposal and everything it entailed, he would not be in this position now. It almost seemed to Rafael that she had taken a stance and then had proceeded to turn herself into a completely different human being. He had thought her perfect wife material: docile, good-natured, uncomplicated, with the added bonus of being very sexy indeed, especially in comparison to his usual diet of stick-thin women. She was, he had thought with satisfaction, the ultimate traditional woman and as such just the sort of person to compliment his demanding lifestyle, to accept his unpredictable work hours with no hint of complaint.

He looked at her now, felt that stirring in him again, and tactfully backed away out of natural reach.

He cursed himself for having been such a fool. He might have known that nothing in life was as simple or as straightforward as it appeared. As they said, there was no such thing as a free lunch.

'Well?' he demanded aggressively, unable to relinquish the sour taste in his mouth when he thought of her getting dressed in the turquoise cling-film with the sole intention of appealing to that toad Goodman.

'Well what?'

Rafael caught himself in the nick of time. He was travelling down a dangerous road. He knew that. He was, above all else, supremely self-controlled and yet here he was, behaving like a kid with a severe temper tantrum.

'Well…' He turned away, in the mood for another glass of wine. 'I came here out of concern. You're new at this game, but if you dress like that…' he informed her bluntly as he poured them both another glass. 'You're going to be sending out all the wrong messages.'

'Rafael…' Cristina remembered how complimentary Anthea had been on the subject of her new wardrobe, and really who was better equipped to judge a woman's wardrobe than another woman? Anthea would have told her if anything she had tried on was wrong. She had been more than frank when it had come to telling her that she looked too round in something, or too drained of colour, or too short, or too *anything else* for that matter. 'Loads of other women dress in tight clothes.'

'Loads of other women don't have your shape.' Rafael thought of the ultra-thin women he had dated. They had certainly worn tight clothes and had looked good, but never as sexy as she did.

'I realise I could lose a few pounds…'

'You misunderstand me.' He swallowed a couple mouthfuls of wine and watched her narrowly over the rim of his glass. 'On you, with your body, tight dresses are a temptation no man in his right mind could resist. You've seen how Goodman couldn't keep his eyes off you, and he wasn't the only guy.'

'You managed all right,' Cristina was horrified to hear herself tell him, and she immediately papered over the gaffe by adding brightly, 'I guess that was because you had your girlfriend there.' The girlfriend he hadn't slept with! Was that because he'd thought, secretly, that she was sexier than the pneumatic blonde? *Hadn't he just said that in a tight dress she was a temptation 'no man in his right mind could resist'?* Her wayward mind happily travelled down this road for a while and then screeched to an abrupt halt when she considered that perhaps it was a question of respect. Perhaps Rafael wasn't leaping into bed with her because he was giving the relationship time to grow and develop and, for Rafael, that would be a really big thing.

'I know you haven't slept with her, but I guess you've just decided to take things slowly?'

Rafael was supremely uninterested in any conversation to do with Cindy. What he really wanted to do was pick up on that stray remark, hurriedly retracted. No. What he *really* wanted to do was rip off that dress and lose himself in that fabulous hourglass body of hers.

'How do you know?' he asked thickly, taking a step towards her while she stumbled back a step, so that for a few seconds they were doing a little dance of advance and retreat.

'Know what?' Cristina squeaked. Her body felt suddenly hot and prickly, and she could feel her nipples tightening, her legs going wobbly. It was almost impossible not to relive that scorching passion that could sweep her away into a universe of her own, impossible for her lips not to feel suddenly dry and her lungs suddenly deprived of air.

'What are you doing?' Cristina asked, fever-ishly aware of the way her wayward body was behaving and of the few inches separating them.

Rafael didn't answer. Instead he drew one lean finger along her collarbone and felt her shudder. 'What makes you think that I wasn't one of those guys watching you?' he murmured, his blue, deep-set eyes gleaming in perfect acknowledgment of her response. She might have put on the dress for Goodman, but right now *he* was the only man on her mind. He could read it from her huge eyes staring at him with mesmerised fascination, from the dilated pupils, and from the way she was mois-tening her lips with the tip of her tongue.

Cristina made a strangulated little sound. Having backed up all of five inches, she now found herself pressed against the counter and thereby at his mercy as he placed his big hands squarely on either side of her, blocking all hope of an exit. Not that she actually *wanted* an exit, a small, wicked voice was whispering in her head. It was horrible and it was humiliating but she was liking this, liking his body so close to hers that she could just reach out and touch him, spread her fingers across his hard, muscled chest.

She closed her eyes and reached up to him, blindly seeking out his mouth while her breasts squashed against his chest. The clingy turquoise dress unzipped at the back. All he had to do was pull it down, all ten inches of it, and her body would be free; she would be able to feel his hand on her bare skin. She would think about the consequences later. Right now every nerve in her body was straining to feel him against her. In her head she had a never-ending train of images that just seemed to go round and round as if on a continual loop. Images of his lips on hers, his dark head at her breasts as he suckled on her nipples, his fingers exploring her body, every yearning, craving inch of it.

She reached behind her with one hand and yanked down the zipper. She was barely conscious of doing it, but it felt good as she wriggled the dress down so that she was now bare from the waist up. No bra. The back was low-cut and, as luck had had it, she didn't possess the right bra for the style and so had decided to do without one. Thanks to Rafael, she was far less self-conscious of her breasts than she used to be.

Rafael had dreamed of this body, a dark dream

which he had done his utmost to shove to the back of his mind and to bury under all the reasons why their relationship had split apart at the seams. But it had been there all along, barely contained in the mental box into which it had been shoved.

This hit him like a sudden blow beneath the belt as his hand came into contact with her flesh. He cupped one of her breasts, rubbed his finger abrasively over the nipple and felt it stiffen under his touch.

Then, like a freight train which you heard approaching in the distance but didn't actually impact until it had rammed right into you, it struck him that she wasn't wearing a bra. She had climbed into this dress with Goodman in mind, not *him*.

In a matter of a few seconds, his mood plummeted into the depths of fury. He couldn't remember why he had come here in the first place. Yes, he had put Goodman off, but had he really thought that the manoeuvre had been anything but a temporary delay? He wondered whether she had responded to him just because she had been feeling horny. Her date had stood her up and he was there.

She had confessed—it now seemed like years ago—that she loved him. Her love had certainly been of a very passing nature if she could slip into this sexy little number in the expectations of going to bed with another man.

Once his thoughts began travelling down that route, they began to consume every corner of his mind.

'I really don't think so, do you?' he said, dropping his hands and turning away, because he knew his weakness with her and it was lust. He didn't want to have even the smallest glimpse of that exquisite body.

His abrupt withdrawal was like a bucket of freezing water thrown over her. Cristina looked at that erect back which smacked of cold dismissal with a sinking heart, then she quickly, with shame, pulled her dress up. She couldn't reach behind her to do up the zipper, not without a minor struggle, and she was heavily conscious of it gaping open behind like a mocking reminder of her willingness to drop all her fast-held principles at a single touch.

'I don't know why I was worried about Goodman taking advantage of you in your dazzling new finery…' He swung round to look at her with distaste. 'You obviously more than know where the revealing outfits are going to take you. God knows, you've probably got the contraceptives in readiness on the bedroom table.'

Cristina, hurt, angry and now feeling manipulated, raised her hand without thinking and hit him hard across the face. She looked in horror first at the stinging palm of her hand, and then at his cheek as the imprint of her fingers slowly formed a red stain across the side of his face. The apology died on her lips when she saw his expression. He was looking at her as if she were something that had crawled out from underneath a rock. He had never looked at her like that, not even when she had handed him back his engagement ring.

'That's…that's a horrible thing to say,' she whispered, but he was already turning away, heading for the door.

She had an insane desire to tug at his shirt and make him stay rather than watch him walk away and leave in his wake this great, ugly pool of bitterness and misunderstanding. Had he kissed her as some kind of *trick*? she wondered feverishly. Had he thought that she had turned over some kind of new leaf, become cheap and easy, the sort of girl who would wear a sexy dress, invite a man back to her apartment and spend the night with him? The sort of girl she had never been and never could be?

She flew behind him and finally, when he was putting on his jacket, she *did* clutch his arm. Hopefully she didn't appear too desperate but she wouldn't have put money on that.

'Please don't go. Not like this.'

Rafael stopped to look coldly at her. 'Not like what?'

'James was just a *date*! I wasn't going to… I'm not *like* that! Why did you kiss me?' She had to know.

'You would have fallen into bed with me.'

'Because you know how I feel about you. I know it would have been a big mistake, but did you just kiss me because you wanted to prove that you *could*? Were you jealous of James?'

'Me? Jealous of *Goodman*?' The mere fact that she had reminded him of a feeling he had no time for, a feeling which was for losers who didn't mind feeling vulnerable—sad sacks who didn't mind handing over the reins of control to someone else—was enough to fuel his anger at her.

'No, of course you wouldn't be,' Cristina said in a strained voice. 'You have Cindy.' He may have lost control for a split second—maybe he had just wanted to put her to the test, to find out whether she was as lacking in self-control as he seemed to think she was—but he had pulled back out of respect for the wonderful woman he still hadn't slept with. She wondered how she could ever have felt uplifted at the thought that he hadn't slept with the blonde. Had she been *mad*? Was it any wonder that he felt sorry for her? It was easy to feel sorry for the person you've left behind when you, yourself, have successfully moved forward with your life.

She hugged herself and stared down at the ground. The high-heeled shoes had been discarded somewhere along the way and, in her stockinged feet, she was as physically disadvantaged as she knew she would be. It was like being in the shadow of a towering volcano. She expected that he was disappointed and disgusted with her. Probably counting his lucky stars that he hadn't ended up with a woman he now, *incor-*

rectly, thought had absolutely no morals. He couldn't have been more wrong but she didn't even know where to begin to tell him that. His face was closed and forbidding, and horribly, *horribly* cold.

'You shouldn't have come here tonight,' she mumbled with heartfelt sincerity.

It was a sentiment with which Rafael wholeheartedly concurred. The thought of her with Goodman—dressing for him, getting ready for him, tempted to sleep with him, whatever she stammered out about not being *that sort of girl*—would live in his head for ever.

'I couldn't agree more,' he told her icily. 'Furthermore, Goodman's welcome to you.'

CHAPTER TEN

THREE days later and Cristina decided that she had to get away. She kept reliving every minute of their last encounter and, the more she relived it, the more hopeless and despairing she felt. She hadn't meant to see him after the party, and when he'd turned up on her doorstep she hadn't meant to let him get physically near her, but she had, and now she couldn't stop beating herself up for her weakness. She had to get over him, and even being in the same city as he was, improbable though it was that she would ever catch sight of him, made her feel a bit panicked.

Anthea would be able to manage the flower shop on her own for a few days. She would leave loads of instructions and she would make sure that she wasn't out of the country, although what she really would have loved to do was to pack her bags and slink back to the warm bosom of her family.

She could easily have rented a room in a hotel and disappeared off to a conveniently remote place, but in the end she telephoned one of the women she had met at the party in connection with a possible landscaping job. It hadn't been anything big, just redoing a tiny bit of their garden at the back where they wanted a useful vegetable plot to be incorporated into something ornamental. Cristina remembered it because it was out in the country and she could be accommodated in a tiny cottage on the estate.

Having had no expectations that she would be in luck, she was pleasantly surprised when Amelia Connolly remembered her, and even more pleasantly surprised to be told that she could come immediately and stay for a few days, which would suit them fine as they were going to be out of the country for a fortnight.

So the following day saw her stepping out of her car and clutching the key to the cottage which she had retrieved from a neighbour, whose house lay out of sight behind fields and towering trees.

The main house was very grand. It was a traditional red-bricked Victorian mansion on a vast scale, and she could easily picture its elegant past of servants and butlers, cooks and nannies. Amelia and her husband had two young children and the house seemed very big for a family of only four, two of whom were only just out of nappies, but then some people just liked having an awful lot of space around them.

The cottage was much more her style. It was at the front of the property, where the long, gravelled drive to the main house began, and it was very picturesque.

Inside not a great deal had been done and it was charming, with a small kitchen, a tiny little snug, and upstairs just the one bedroom and bathroom.

Cristina decided that she would explore the grounds in the morning because she was exhausted, even though the trip up had taken a scant two hours in her little car. She could hardly remember when she had last slept well; the past couple of nights had been a disaster. She had taken ages to fall asleep, and when she eventually had she had been awakened by dreams, which had all involved variations of Rafael vanishing into the distance while she tried to follow him only to discover that her feet were cemented to the ground.

She had brought enough food to last four days, which was how long she intended on staying. But, opening the fridge, she saw that Amelia had kindly stocked up with the basics, and beside a little dish of eggs on the counter was a note telling her to make herself at home, as well as several sheaths of paper detailing what sort of ideas they had for the vegetable plot.

Dinner was a cheese omelette, and by the time eight-thirty rolled around she was ready to fall asleep in front of the television. The mere fact that she wasn't in London was good for her mind. Yes, she still thought of Rafael as she lay in bed with her eyes closed, but at least he didn't pursue her in her dreams as well. And the following day she was bright-eyed and ready to start having a look at her project.

Losing herself in the maintained gardens and woodland was very easy for Cristina to do. More than once she wondered what on earth had possessed her to settle in London. When had it ever been her life's ambition to live in a city surrounded by pollution, traffic and constant noise? She decided that she really would think about moving somewhere, where the views were not impeded by buildings, or the only greenery was contained in parks which were only ever bearable in winter when no one else was interested in using them.

Because of the acres of land to explore, Cristina had packed herself a picnic lunch, and it was absolute heaven sitting on the edge of the woodland, a small copse fragrant with lavender which was all part of the estate.

She was in no rush to get back to the cottage. It was gloriously warm and she could have remained outdoors for ever. The wide open space was a soothing balm for her fretful mind. Frankly, she would have spent the night outdoors if she wasn't slightly spooked by a comment Amelia had made about being glad to have someone around who could 'keep their eyes on things'. Cristina knew she had been joking, but still had visions of gangs of teenagers joy riding along the narrow country lanes, high on drink and drugs, and chancing upon her sleeping under a tree outside because she had fancied being at one with nature. She was pretty sure that she had seen a movie along those lines, and it had been scary enough on celluloid. She wasn't going to risk the real thing for the sake of a night under the stars.

But by the time she had eaten her lunch and had a nap, something she never did in London, and then had busied herself sitting out in the open fields with her A4 pads, her graph paper, her pencils and her gardening books, it was nearly eight and the light was beginning to fade.

It had been a busy, enjoyable and productive day, and she was hopeful that she would literally fall into bed and be asleep within minutes. In her mind, indications warranting a very large tick in the 'recovery and forgetting Rafael' box included getting into bed and falling asleep within minutes.

There was no warning at all by the time she finally made it back that anyone was in the cottage aside from herself. The door was unlocked, but then she remembered leaving it that way because she hadn't planned on being out for as long as she had, nor had she planned on straying as far from the cottage as she had ended up doing.

She went into the kitchen, switched on the light, dumped her stuff on the pine kitchen-table and was only aware of another presence by the shadow from behind her. A very big shadow. A shadow announcing a prowler who had made no noise whatsoever as he had entered the kitchen behind her.

Cristina didn't stop to think. She swung round with her gardening book, and there was a satisfying thud as it made swift and violent contact with the intruder.

Rafael buckled under the vigour of the attack and the element of surprise. He had been forced to park outside the estate because the imposing front gates were locked, had braved the brick wall, clambering foliage and hedges, keenly aware that small country lanes were frequented by do-good ramblers who'd have thought nothing of setting their mutts onto him should they get the slightest whiff that he'd been planning to sneak into the grounds of the local gentry.

But he had made it in two hours previously and had found the cottage open but empty. He had contemplated walking the grounds in search of her but, first things first, he had had to have a shower because he'd been scratched, bleeding in places and filthy. And, with his trousers and shirt no longer of any use to man nor beast, he had been reduced to his boxers and the pink dressing-gown which she had brought with her and which had been hanging on a hook behind the bedroom door. It was too short, too small to be belted in any way, too pink, and made him resemble a cartoon character, but it would be less scary than the sight of him, unannounced, in nothing but his underwear.

Rafael, a man who could inspire fear without saying a word, was floundering in unknown territory, and he was a hell of a lot less fazed by the ridiculous figure he cut than he was by the knowledge that he was capable of being scared—that he *was* scared—scared that she might turn her back on him and walk away.

Cristina's first reaction as Rafael doubled over was *why is this large, strange man wearing my bathrobe?* Then she registered the identity of the intruder and stepped back in shock, but her shock, lasting only a few seconds, was replaced by hot, acid bitterness that filled her throat and made her feel literally sick.

She watched him coldly, her arms folded, as he slowly regained his breath and gradually stood up. 'How did you find out where I was?'

Rafael rubbed his ribs where she had smashed

him with the gardening manual. It must weigh a ton, and she had spared no effort. On a better day he might have joked that the Territorial Army could find her a real asset.

'I managed to persuade your friend at the flower shop that it was in your best interests that I find out where you were staying. How much does that book weigh anyway? I think you may have broken a couple of my ribs.' It was a weak attempt at a joke, and it fell as flat as a lead balloon. He looked at her icy expression and felt another knot of sickening fear in the pit of his stomach.

'Good, because you shouldn't be here, and I want you to leave. I want you to take off my bathrobe and just get out of my life.'

'Don't say that, Cristina. Please.'

He had that voice that could make her go weak at the knees, but she found that they felt remarkably steady at the moment. The past, she thought, couldn't be buried under a *please*. She didn't even know why he was here and she wasn't going to ask so she remained silent, looking at him, her whole mind taken up with the nightmare of that last conversation they had had.

'I… Problem with the clothes…' He gestured

to the robe. 'My clothes are soaking in the bath upstairs…' Did she want to find out *why*? It would appear not, because she just kept her eyes focused icily on him. For someone who was naturally such a sunny personality, whose face was truly a mirror into her thoughts, that lack of expression was as powerfully offputting as any shouting ever could have been.

'I…I couldn't get in,' Rafael expanded into the devouring silence. 'The gates were locked so I had to find a spot in the wall to climb over. Only problem was that I had to do a bit of battle with overhanging trees and dense hedge. Hence the outfit.' He paused, waiting for her to show some interest in what he was saying and knowing that she wouldn't. 'Fortunately the front door to the cottage was open so I could get cleaned up inside. Aren't you going to ask me what I'm doing here?'

'Tell me why I should care, Rafael?'

'This isn't easy for me.'

'What isn't? Look, I don't want any more arguments with you, and I don't want you reappearing in my life whenever you feel like it.'

'I understand that.'

'No, you don't, Rafael!' She could feel her whole body shaking at the thought of him standing here in front of her, wrecking her nervous system, just when she'd been beginning to feel a little stronger. Was he going to keep on doing that—checking up on her whenever he was at loose ends? Whenever his conscience decided to rebel? Maybe he felt that he just *could* because he figured that he was her weakness, her Achilles' heel, and therefore he could dip in and out of her life as the fancy took him. 'The last time we spoke…'

'Please, hear me out at least.' *Why the hell should she?* He had hurt her deeply. Was it any surprise that she could barely look at him? The urgency of needing her to listen struck him with the force of a tidal wave, made his legs feel a little shaky. On the drive up, he had planned how this conversation would go. Generally speaking, he would emerge cool, controlled, a big guy willing to admit mistakes and generous enough to express his feelings in a manner that was not namby pamby or loser-like. Three minutes in and he had lost it. She was looking at him as if he were something that had crawled out from under a rock and was now threatening to infect her.

Dulled colour highlighted his sharp cheek-bones. He found that he might be better off sitting down.

'Look, there's something you should know. Goodman. I did it. Phoned him up. Knew that he had made plans to see you. Also made sure that those plans came to nothing.' He leaned forward, resting his elbows on his knees.

'You did *what*?'

'I was jealous!' He glared at her, his expression telling her that there was nothing else he could have done given the circumstances, but it fell on stony ground.

'Not content in messing up my life, you actually decided that you would eliminate the first guy who might just be interested in me?'

'Okay, so maybe I was out of order.'

'Maybe?'

'But I've never been a jealous man, never had any cause to be.'

Cristina knew why he was jealous. She had been *his* possession, the *chosen one,* and his ego hadn't been able to bear the indignity of her messing up his carefully laid plans and, worse, possibly sparking up a relationship with one of his buddies.

'It's all about *you*, isn't it, Rafael? *You* decide that it's time to find yourself a suitable wife, *you* pick the person and lay down all the ground rules, *you* react like a kid who hasn't got his Christmas present when your arrangements don't go according to plan!'

'Yes.'

Cristina blinked. Had he just *agreed* with her or had she imagined that? 'What did you just say?'

'You're right. It was all about me.' He looked at her, watched as she warily sat on the chair facing him, wondered whether this was a good sign or not, and then decided that he wouldn't even go there; he had made enough mistakes already, been way too arrogant, and had paid the price. 'I wasn't thinking of you when I made my plans, wasn't thinking about what you might like or not like. I took you for granted, and assumed that you would fall into line with a marriage because it made sense on paper.'

'And suddenly you've had an epiphany?' Cristina laughed humourlessly. 'You really expect me to believe that you've changed miraculously overnight?'

'I… No… I don't expect anything.'

Cristina was momentarily disconcerted by his humility. Was it for real? Was he that good an actor? She felt battered by sudden, dreadful hope, and had to grit her teeth together because hope, as she had discovered, was the mortal enemy of reality.

'I…I never thought that I could feel that urgency and passion again, that thing I once called *love*. I had had that with my ex-wife, and I had seen first-hand how easily it could dissolve. I had spent my years quite happy to go from one relationship to another. But here's the thing—what I felt for Helen was never love. And to answer your question, no, I didn't have a sudden epiphany. I just realised that what I felt for you had sneaked up on me, and without even knowing it I could no longer survive without you. I figured that it was a happy coincidence that we got along, a happy coincidence we were compatible, sheer good luck that aside from our similar backgrounds it was all so effortless being in your company…' He raked his fingers through his hair and Cristina saw, to her amazement, that his hand was shaking. This was being wrenched out of him and that, more than anything else, gave her pause for thought.

'I didn't understand what you meant to me until you had gone, and even then I couldn't admit that I had fallen in love with you. I just thought…I just thought that it was fine if you wanted to walk away because I was immune to being hurt. My head said so. I don't want to marry you because you fit the bill, Cristina. I want to marry you because I can't survive without you. I'm crazy with jealousy over every man you talk to. Watching you at my party, flirting with Goodman…it was torture. I could have hit him.'

Cristina felt the pain of sudden, fierce tenderness. She had seen many sides of Rafael, but this side, the vulnerable man tentatively working his way through his feelings, allowing her to see his fear and uncertainty, was the most powerful indication of his sincerity.

'So will you marry me, Cristina?' He looked at her, feeling that there was a heck of a lot more to say, and knowing that gradually, over time, if she had him, he would tell her how he felt and would never stop telling her. Right now he had only just covered the tip of the iceberg. 'I can't live without your laugh. You put perspective in my life, Cristina, and if you can't give me an answer now then I'll wait, even if it means waiting for the rest of my life.'

'You won't have to wait, Rafael. I can give you my answer right now…'

EPILOGUE

ONE YEAR LATER AND this time round the occasion at his mother's house was of a different sort. Both families had met for the wedding in Italy, which had been a small affair, according to Cristina's wishes. This time, they were meeting for the christening of the first Rocchi grandchild, a beautiful little girl conceived shortly after their glorious honeymoon in the Seychelles. And, as Rafael had smugly pointed out to her, appropriately conceived in their new house, a charming Grade II listed cottage far enough out of London to feel rural, but not so far that he couldn't get to London if he had to.

It had all the features Cristina had yearned for in a house: the clambering roses, the white picket fence, the orchard at the back. There were fireplaces for open fires, beams galore, and a kitchen that could make a chef out of anyone because

Rafael had seen to it that it had been kitted out to the highest possible standard.

And the trump card was the picturesque little village with its picture-postcard village green, cricket ground and corner pub. There, Cristina had set up her little flower shop and landscaping services, and Anthea had been all too happy to move to the area and become joint partner in the enterprise.

Life had never been better.

Rafael looked at his beloved wife cradling their baby daughter, as friends and relatives ooh-ed and aah-ed, and he walked across to gently kiss the top of her head.

'Stunning, isn't she?' He addressed the assembled audience of five with a satisfied smile, his arm loosely around Cristina's shoulders. 'Everyone says,' he solemnly told them, 'She is the spitting image of her father...' He felt his wife laugh and grinned down at her and the perfect rosy-cheeked face of his baby daughter with her miniature fist clenched by her mouth. 'Which is why she wants to have at least four more...set the balance straight, so to speak...' He wanted at least four; she had laughed and told him that he might very well be singing a different tune if he had had to undergo the pregnancy and birth, but he knew that she had loved every minute of being pregnant, and that the idea of a house filled with children was as appealing for her as it was for him.

Cristina felt the weight of his arm around her and relaxed into the casual embrace. He had never stopped telling her how much he loved her, and Isabella Maria had proved that, not only could he be an amazing husband, he could also be an amazing and doting father.

'And…' he bent so that he could whisper into her ear '…my darling, I can't wait for everyone to leave so that we can start trying…'

MILLS & BOON PUBLISH EIGHT LARGE PRINT TITLES A MONTH. THESE ARE THE EIGHT TITLES FOR MARCH 2009.

RUTHLESSLY BEDDED BY THE ITALIAN BILLIONAIRE
Emma Darcy

MENDEZ'S MISTRESS
Anne Mather

RAFAEL'S SUITABLE BRIDE
Cathy Williams

DESERT PRINCE, DEFIANT VIRGIN
Kim Lawrence

WEDDED IN A WHIRLWIND
Liz Fielding

BLIND DATE WITH THE BOSS
Barbara Hannay

THE TYCOON'S CHRISTMAS PROPOSAL
Jackie Braun

CHRISTMAS WISHES, MISTLETOE KISSES
Fiona Harper

MILLS & BOON®
Pure reading pleasure™

0309 Rom LP

MILLS & BOON PUBLISH EIGHT LARGE PRINT TITLES A MONTH. THESE ARE THE EIGHT TITLES FOR APRIL 2009.

THE GREEK TYCOON'S DISOBEDIENT BRIDE
Lynne Graham

THE VENETIAN'S MIDNIGHT MISTRESS
Carole Mortimer

RUTHLESS TYCOON, INNOCENT WIFE
Helen Brooks

THE SHEIKH'S WAYWARD WIFE
Sandra Marton

THE ITALIAN'S CHRISTMAS MIRACLE
Lucy Gordon

CINDERELLA AND THE COWBOY
Judy Christenberry

HIS MISTLETOE BRIDE
Cara Colter

PREGNANT: FATHER WANTED
Claire Baxter

MILLS & BOON®
Pure reading pleasure™